Safe at Home

A 1Night Stand Story

By
Wendy Burke

Copyright © 2016 by Wendy Burke
ISBN: 978-1-68361-095-3
Cover art by Fiona Jayde

Published by
Decadent Publishing Company, LLC

Look for us online at:
www.decadentpublishing.com

~A Note from the Author~

Whether Miller Park in my home state of Wisconsin, or Comerica Park near my current home of Ohio, or Fifth Third Field home of the world famous Toledo Mud Hens in my adopted hometown of Toledo, some of my best days have been in the stands of a ball park. And, whenever at a game, I make sure to tip a beer to an old friend, gone now more than a decade. I never cheered louder, laughed more heartily or felt more "at home" than with you, Debbie Guenther. I miss those wonderful days in the 70s and 80s in the bleachers of Milwaukee County Stadium, or when we'd splurge and for $14 get box seats behind home plate. Life was easier, simpler and much more innocent. I miss you every day, my friend!

Wendy Burke

Dedication

Thanks a bunch to:

You! —who decided to spend a couple bucks on some silly rantings which came out of my head. *Thank You!* Go ahead and holler at me: wendyburke1994@bex.net.

'The Huz' – even though you may not understand what's going on in my head, you love and support me and every one of these endeavors just the same. (And, no, I didn't kill you off in the first six pages of the first book I wrote!)

My 'partner-in-1Night Stand crime,' Deanna Wadsworth – for the butt-kicking, critiquing, beta-reading, talking me out of a tree, stealing my characters, forcing me to be a better writer, putting Sam Adams Lite in my hair, and so much more.

Jill Kemerer – for being the wonderful, sweet encourager you are! Lunch is on *me* next time. (You look fabulous on TV!)

Val & the DP Gang – you freed the people in my head! (Even now, I'm sure you're editing those em-dashes!)

Louie, Maximus the Gladiator Kitten, and Sir Wolfie T. Fluffernutter – none of you can read, but you all spent a lot of encouraging time on my laptop. My life is so much more fun with the three of you.

And the following folks in no particular order, who may or may not know your contribution to my madness: D.B.; the gang on the 'Party Line' for always 'going there'; the newsroom conspirators and 'input artists' - Darla, Allie, Alicia, Corey, Jared, Jimmie, Ali, Amanda, and yes, even 'Babe' (my apologies if I left out anyone!)

Chapter One

"*Un moment, s'il vous plait.*" Charly Knox dropped her cell phone on her desk and stared slack-jawed at the muted television. The off-season report on ESPN *couldn't* be true! Her husband's handsome face was on the screen, the word *GONE* flashing above the shortstop's image, after which red question marks danced across the screen. She didn't bother to turn up the volume. She'd seen the bad news and certainly didn't want to *hear* it.

Stunned, she retrieved her phone and brought it back to her ear. "Josef, *mon cher*, I'm going to have to call you back." Without a thought, she hit "end," cutting off her boss's boyfriend and stalling a potential six-figure sale of modern art.

"He can't be traded," she said aloud to no one. Dropping into her chair, she scrambled for paper and pen and began the math problem. "Four and half years in Milwaukee, a half season in Minnesota, back to the Breakers...crap." The numbers didn't add up—Andy hadn't played ten years in the major leagues nor had five consecutive seasons with the same team. Sighing, the weight of the situation began to settle. "He doesn't meet the union criteria to refuse the trade."

Text after text rolled across the screen of her cell. The *WTF?* and *Call me ASAP!* messages added to her irritation.

"What the eff is right. Not even a heads-up?" Closing her eyes for a moment, she realized she'd been left in the dark by the one man she completely trusted with her life, her husband, shortstop for the Milwaukee Breakers, Andy Knox. Staring out the large bay window at the expansive snow-covered backyard, she allowed her thoughts to wander.

"Mommy?"

The little voice brought her back to reality. "Yeah, baby?"

Damn, how long has Bree been standing there?

Never far from one another, Bree and her four-year-old twin sister stood in the doorway. Chloe held up a receiver. "The telephone, Momma."

She hadn't even noticed the rarely-used landline phone ringing. Shaking off the emotional overload, she ousted thoughts of leaving her house and the home state she loved, and picked up the phone. "Thank you, Chloe. Hello?"

"Need anything from the store, hon?"

Andy's voice covered her like a warm blanket fresh from the dryer. Her confusion and slight ire dissipated with his tone. "Uh, no. I don't think so."

"Okay. I finished up in the cage and stopped off at Ray's office."

Keep it under your hat until you can talk to him face to face. "How *is* that agent of yours?" she prodded, hoping he'd give up something, anything.

"Makin' us money, honey. I gotta keep you in the lifestyle to which you've grown accustomed!" he joked.

She teased back. "I work for a living, remember? I made more money than you did for *quite* some time, Mr. Sarasota Sea Turtle!"

"Wow...kind of early for your period, isn't it?" he snickered.

"I guess that was a low blow, huh?"

"Maybe, but I like it when you blow...."

"Stop it. The girls are right here!"

"Give them the phone. I'll talk to them so you can go sell shit I don't understand. I'll be home in a bit. Love you."

"Love you, too. Here's Bree."

Turning the phone back over her older child, Bree punched the button to put the phone on speaker, and the girls took their conversation with their father into another part of the house.

Toddlers and technology...they know more than I do!

Charly's cell phone continued its symphony of pings and rumbles. When the friendly face of her boss, owner of Third Street Gallery, appeared on caller ID, she had to answer. "Paulie, please apologize to Josef for me, I didn't mean to be so abrupt."

"He was just concerned, darling. After the phone went dead, we both texted and called with no reply. Everything all right? The girls okay?"

Not wanting to give too much away, she fibbed. "Yes, sure. Everything is fine. I got distracted by something."

"Well, don't be late. You know the Gallery doesn't *run* without you, love."

"Thanks, Paulie. Bye." She tossed her phone aside, letting the nearly perpetual texts scroll across the screen, unread.

Sighing, she took stock of the situation and hoped she could curb her simmering irritation. Her husband had obviously kept her out of his professional loop. The question was why. Clutching the tiny diamond cross at the end of her necklace, Charly looked toward the ceiling and begged. "Please, God, anywhere but New York."

***

Andy waited for the words "call ended" to appear on the dashboard console. After stopping at his agent's office, for nearly an hour he'd sat in his pickup staring out the windshield at the ice on Lake Michigan. "This is gonna suck...bad...." But at this point, there was no way around it. The information he had to break to his wife, his best *friend* since high school, was already out there for the whole world to see and speculate upon. He was being traded. But that wasn't the worst of it.

He lifted the overstuffed manila envelope from the passenger seat and pulled out just enough of the paperwork to see the first paragraph of his newest contract. Three words mid-way through the first sentence stared back at him. *New York Titans*. Taking a centering breath and girding his bravery for what he knew would come, he stuffed his future back into the envelope.

"She's gonna kill me." Putting the truck in gear, reluctantly he headed for home.

***

"Daddy's home!"

He was barely in the mudroom from the garage when his daughters assaulted him, wrapping their arms about his legs and clinging to him for dear life. "Whoa!" He grabbed onto the waistband of his sweats, before they were unintentionally yanked from his legs. Looking into the kitchen, he watched Charly shake her head at the silliness.

The girls clenched tightly to his legs, giggling happily as he schlepped up to where his wife poured coffee into a travel mug.

"Hey, baby." He kissed her cheek.

"Hey, yourself." She looked down at her children, "Ladies, go pick out your clothes, so Daddy can get you dressed. I have to go to Uncle Paul's store for a little while."

Andy bent down, kissed their heads, and patted their little butts before they disappeared out of his reach. "How do you get them to do that?" Turning back to his wife and slipping his arms about her middle, he rested his chin on her shoulder.

"Do what?"

"You say jump and they ask how high?"

Her trim form turned in his hold. The short fluff of her cashmere sweater tickled his neck. "Because they know I run the show here."

Hugging her tightly, he picked up her familiar scent, which, even after all these years, stirred him. "You do, huh?"

"At least that's what I'm told." She leaned slightly out of his hold. "What did Ray have to say?"

He knew her beautiful smile would disappear in mere moments. "I've been dealt."

"Well, you must've been the *last* to know. It's all over ESPN, and my phone's been blowing up all morning. Why didn't you tell me, Andy?" She forced her way out of his embrace, turning her back on him. She went back to readying her coffee.

"I've been meaning to, but I wanted to get more details first."

"Where to?"

"That's still up in the air," he fibbed. "Guess I'm part of some multi-team deal."

Andy watched her slow turn, the happy-to-see-him smile on her face gone, replaced with a serious expression. Her voice took on an I've-been-around-this-business-almost-as-long-as-you-have tone. "That sort of maneuvering doesn't happen overnight. How long has this been in the works?"

"Couple weeks I guess."

"Really, Andy?" Rarely did she get mad, but he could see a storm brewing in his wife's gray eyes.

"C'mere." Taking her hand, he drew her over to a kitchen chair. Sitting down in front of her, he took her hands and leaned in for a conversation of somewhat half-truths. "We don't have to move."

"That's the least of my concerns, right now. What a crappy way to find out. I got the news the same moment the entire viewership of

ESPN did, and I'm *married* to the player being traded. Why did you keep this from me?"

"I didn't, babe. Wanted to get all my ducks in a row first. *I'm* dealing with this, too, you know."

They sighed, practically in unison, and in the same emotional tone. That happened after nearly ten years of marriage and almost fifteen of being together.

"I'm not crazy about this situation either." Leaning in, he put his forehead to hers. "*This* is home, always has been." And it was. The two had met in a high school English class fewer than forty miles from where they now sat.

"But...."

"But, we both know I'm too young...."

"And too good," she added.

He smiled, thanking God that even through her irritation she understood he had many more years left to play. "And healthy to retire. And, it's provided well for us and the girls. So let's see where this goes and we'll deal with it, okay?"

***

Hunkered down on the sectional in the back of the gallery, Charly sat knee-to-knee with artist Emmy Klaussen. The glass designer nodded and handed over tissue after tissue as Charly explained her predicament. They looked up as the shop's owner entered.

"Ladies, what is going on here?" Paul Strait asked.

"Andy's getting traded."

"Oh, is *that* all, Charly? For a moment, I thought someone had died!"

"You're an asshole, Pauly," Emmy mumbled.

"I know, that's why Josef loves me so."

Charly rolled her eyes and sighed. Since Paul had met the Haitian sculptor through the 1Night Stand agency owned by some mysterious Madame Eve, his attitude and life had changed for the better. Sometimes, however, hearing about all that elation got old. Once in a while everyone had to deal with less-than-blissful reality.

He plopped down next to the women. "Please stop with the tears, you look like one of those *starving artists* vendors in some tacky hotel ballroom trying to hawk knock offs and prints." He put his hand on Charly's knee. "So, what *do* we know?"

"All I know I found out watching *Sports Center* this morning. He didn't even bother to tell me first. That sucked. He says he doesn't know where he's going yet. I don't know what we're going to do."

Emmy put her arms about Charly's shoulders and gave her a hearty hug. "After all these years of knowing you, I think you're kind of acting like a spoiled, affluent prima donna. It's not like he's getting shipped to a war zone." Kissing her on the top of the head, Emmy left employer and employee to themselves.

"I love her. She doesn't mince words, does she?" Charly said quietly.

"Compared to what she went through, you know, you don't have much to worry about."

Charly understood. Emmy had raised a son with Paul's assistance and the help of her family, as she waited to find out if her missing fiancé was dead or alive. Along with help from 1Night Stand, kismet had smiled on the couple. Nick Klaussen returned from the first Gulf War alive, and the lovers had been reunited, even if twenty years had separated them.

Charly's situation, by comparison, was nothing. What was a few hundred miles in first class then settling in to five star digs wherever she visited her Major League hubby?

Paul waved a hand at her. "Go home."

"Are you kidding? *You're* not going to unpack and set up the new exhibits!"

"Your mind isn't here, honey, it's at home with that six-foot-three *god* of a baseball player. Go home, and spend the day in bed with that hot shortstop of yours."

She shrugged at him. "Well, if you insist!"

***

No other sound compared to the elated shrieks of her children. Charly could hear giggling and happy laughter over the house-filling volume of singing and the strumming of a twelve-string. The girls' tiny voices mixed with their father's country-crooner tone. Hanging her coat, Charly leaned against the wall of the foyer. She sighed, warming at her husband's sexy voice. His serenade had lulled her to sleep after the first time they'd made love. If Andy hadn't been so good at baseball, a singing career in Nashville would have been a viable option.

She swallowed hard. Of course, today's news bothered her, but an underlying, unidentified worry also poked at her.

"Mommy!" Breanna, the six-minutes-older of their two girls, ran headlong into her legs. "Can you hear Daddy singing?"

"Yes, I can," she said, ruffling the girl's light-brown hair. She swung her daughter up into her hold, continuing her trek toward the music. She waited in the doorway, watching her husband and second born, Chloe, in her father's embrace. He held her little fingers to the fret of his guitar, strumming. Chloe cocked her head, listening as the sound changed. Music or art, Charly didn't care which they pursued as long as their girls understood the inherent beauty in everything in the world.

"Mommy's home," Chloe mentioned to her father.

"Home so soon, babe?" he asked.

Placing her daughter on the floor, she patted Bree's little butt. "Why don't you and Chloe go play in your room, so Mommy and Daddy can talk."

Chloe slid out of her father's lap. "So you and Mommy can do those yucky kisses," she mumbled under her breath, and trotted after her sister to another part of the house.

Once the girls had left, Charly wandered over to the couch and straddled her husband's lap. A bright smile lit up his face. "What is it, hon?"

His melted-chocolate brown eyes sparkled. Just looking at him made her want to grab his hand and haul him off to the bedroom. "Paul sent me home."

She knew he could read her, he always could. Like she could read him, and always had. "I don't know, I guess I'm still in a bit of shock. I mean, we're so comfortable here. This is *home,* and I don't want to leave again." She didn't want to cry, yet one giant, unexpected tear cascaded down her cheek.

He kissed her forehead then rested his face in her neck. "This *is* home and will always be." A lustful shiver went through her as the light scruff on his cheeks prickled her neck. With an enticing nip of her earlobe, he asked, "Don't tell me. Paul said we should spend the day in bed, right?"

"He did, but I should have stayed at work. We have a couple of new pieces coming in, and I should be there to figure out how to display them...."

She knew what his reaction would be. No sooner had she started talking about her work than he checked out, his head dropping to her shoulder with a sigh.

She popped him lightly on the shoulder. "Andy!" He lifted his head from her sweater. "Are you listening to me?"

His hands surrounded her face, and he kissed her gently on the mouth. "I'm sorry, honey. You know that art talk gets me all glazed over."

One tiny kiss. That's an apology? Just once, Andrew, if you could only pretend to be interested. Before we were married, you at least tried! She swallowed her irritation and left his lap. She hadn't moved far when he stopped her. Andy's strong arms wrapped about her waist, holding her close.

"About that day in bed," he breathed in her ear.

Nodding, she forgave his "art inattentiveness," relented, and waited for her stunning specimen of a husband to carry her off to an afternoon of unmatched orgasms. He was reaching to scoop her up into his arms, when two still pajama-clad four year olds blocked his path.

"Your fancy phone, Daddy. You left it in the living room." Bree held the device up to him.

"The phone is ringing. The phone is ringing," Chloe sang. "You have to answer the phone!" Then with a piercing whoop only a tot's small voice box could elicit, "Daddy, answer the phone!"

"Geez, now I *do* have a headache," she whispered. She encouraged her husband to release her, and kissed his cheek, "You owe me one." Taking the phone from Chloe, she gave a sour look at the caller ID and handed over the device. She smiled at their daughters. "I think two young ladies need to brush their teeth," she said, leaving Andy alone with the phone.

Chapter Two

"All right, have your minion bring the paperwork over. We'll be here all day," Andy said to his agent on the phone. "Ah, no, I'm sure she's not going to be thrilled...not even with a contract of that size. You know it's not about the money...yes, I'll smooch her for you, but I'm thinking you'd better drop into the gallery and buy something. This time around I'm *sure* she won't give you the friends and family discount....all right...and one more thing. The details *do not* hit the media until late tomorrow. Can you make that happen? All right. Yes, bye."

He hit end, wandered over to his desk, and dropped into the chair. He looked at all the Milwaukee Breakers memorabilia. His first big-league jersey hung on the wall in a dark-wood frame. The back faced outward, his number—twenty-seven—and Knox embroidered in the Breaker's signature dark-blue. As a New York Titan, spring training would move from Phoenix east to Tampa. Technically, Tampa was closer to home, but he still knew Charly wouldn't relish any of the changes this trade would involve. *I can sugarcoat it.* She had friends and family in Florida. Her boss had recently opened a gallery in Miami and her Aunt Rita had moved there, too. Andy knew his wife fit in anywhere, so hanging with Titan wives and girlfriends shouldn't be a problem. *Who am I kidding? She's gonna hate every minute of it and I don't blame her.* He couldn't even convince himself.

He visited with all the professional *stuff* he'd accumulated over the years—the first grand slam ball hit in his home stadium; an inside-the-park homerun ball, also struck inside the Milwaukee stadium; a photo of him, hovering above second base, ball in glove, a tap on an opponent's helmet, the turn of a triple play, and guess what? Again, inside the Milwaukee Park.

Giving up a resigned sigh, he swallowed hard. He knew she'd despise it, but hoped his wife would get accustomed to him wearing Titan pinstripes.

***

"We can stay home if you want to."

"No, you promised you'd play that bar with the guys. It's fine." She wandered up to the bathroom sink, watching him ever so slightly spike up his short, dark hair. Wrapping her arms about his trim, strong middle, she hugged him, feeling the ripples of his well-worked abs under her fingers. Her cheek on his back, she whispered, "I love you."

Andy's warm, callused hands surrounded hers. His tone was quiet, understanding. "I know today's news is hard to take...."

She squeezed him, not wanting to talk about *his* impending move any more today. "It is, but let's forget about it for now. I'll decide how upset I need to be when I find out where you're going, how far away you'll be, and how often you'll be able to be home." She shivered when he kissed her fingers. Charly knew he understood her concerns. "So, let's leave the rest of this conversation for another time."

He turned in her hold. Looking at her, he pulled his fingers across his lips, securing an invisible zipper, and then tossed away its locking key.

Holding him tightly, she rubbed her face in his chest. His fresh aroma turned her on more than he'd ever know. At this moment, nothing could touch her; no hurt, no loneliness, no heartache, no curt words from a fan could harm her. She closed and locked the door to any bad memories, especially those from that time when things between them had been emotionally tenuous. For a time before they married, when their relationship had taken a nearly irreparable turn. And at times like this, the same fears, the same insecurities reared up in Charly's mind. Right now though, she was safe and she was home. The man she loved held her tightly in his arms and his lips pressed her cheek.

Maybe she *needed* a night out watching her friend and life partner sing with his buddies, drink a few beers, and have some simple, uncomplicated fun. With a grin, she looked into his face. She *completely* understood why fourteen- to forty-year-olds either were stunned silent or squealed in his presence. He'd always had a great shape, but now, at this point in his career, his body was athletic, toned, cut, fast—a finely tuned machine of muscle, responsive agility and power. But what Charly found most attractive was how he carried himself—sure, strong and commanding, yet with a gentleness, an approachability. His warm, inviting grin put people at ease, invited them into the conversation, and always left *them* feeling *they'd* been the center of attention. His personality completed and complemented him. A truly good-looking intelligent, athletic, loving man, first devoted and in love with his family, second, devoted and in love with the game he treasured, baseball. Charly refocused her fears onto those things she knew and admired about Andy, the man she'd loved for more than half her life.

Looking up into his big, chocolate brown eyes, she smiled again. "Will you do your little dance for me tonight?"

He pursed her lips at her. Sliding his hands down her backside, he gripped her ass firmly and ground his towel-draped groin against her. "The G-rated public version of *this* one?"

She moaned into him. "Uh, huh...it's fun to watch the women in the crowd watch you. I know what they're thinking, and I'm the one who can take advantage of your male stripper gyrating later."

"You can or you *will*?"

"*Will*, I hope."

"You don't' have to *hope,* honey. Trust me, you're the *only one* who gets the *private* show."

***

Charly got a beer and settled in at a table. She watched Andy getting organized with his bandmates. She shook her head, amused. Playing with his buddies, he reminded her of the seventeen-year-old who had goaded her into a date. He dressed the part as well—washed-out long-sleeved T-shirt, ratty backwards ball cap, well-faded trim blue jeans with worn and worn-through spots in all the right places.

Charly smiled—genuinely, for the first time today—watching him and his pals take the small stage. He didn't *walk* up to it, he *popped* with light energy. *I could watch that ass all day and never tire of it.* He carried a microphone with as much ease as he worked a Louisville Slugger. She shook her head, quickly looking away from his gaze as he winked at her. She *knew* the show he'd give, the songs he would sing, the jokes he would tell, but the only thought in her head was the ultra-private show he would give her later.

"Hey, Charlotte Knox!"

Charly spotted one of Andy's soon-to-be-former teammates, Tom Gorman, and waved hello in return. *And, who's that? Certainly* not *your wife with her hand in your back pocket. At least take off your wedding ring!* He winked at her then brought his hand to the side of his face in the international sign for "call me." Still smiling at him, she jokingly shooed him and his lurid flirtations away. *Maybe this trade isn't such a bad thing, if it gets Andy away from* him.

She'd never told anyone and *definitely* not her husband, but once after a small party celebrating the Breakers' lock into post-season play, Tom had hugged her good night and whispered in her ear, "I'm going to miss your pants," making his play and point clear with a solid grasp of her butt. She'd put it out of her mind, chalking it up to alcohol, but seeing her husband's handsome teammate with a woman other than his wife, she knew exactly what he had implied. His blatant adultery bothered her on so many levels. For starters, infidelity was unacceptable; but on a deeper level, Tom physically resembled her father. Seeing Tom with another woman felt like watching her father cheat on her mother—which Charly's father had done frequently, outwardly, and nastily. The only thing more irritating than her dad's blatant adultery was the way he ignored his family, leaving her to care for her hurt, lonely, and ill mother.

She shook the ugly memory from her mind, said a prayer for her mom, and went back to the amazing scenery in front of her. She had no problem being left to her own thoughts, specifically those about her husband on stage. *Just move it, darlin'!* Between his tight, trim ass in somewhat loose jeans and his hips grinding to the beat, it was impossible *not* to be wet.

It seemed he kept a closer eye on her tonight, directing songs and gestures more so in her direction than anyone else's. *Nothing like a little "private" public attention.* When their eyes met, Charly hoped he could read what she thought.

She knew him well enough to guess that he knew exactly the effect he was having on her.

The opening chords of a particularly catchy tune began, and Andy made his way from the stage, slapping hands and spreading fist-bumps in the crowd. Her heart double-clutched as he stopped where she sat. He took her hand, drawing her into his hold. His voice rang in her ear and through the bar's sound system. She swore everyone could see the wet spot on the seat of her prairie skirt.

Holding back a gasp at the intensity of her attraction to him, Charly swayed against him, his trim, solid leg nudging between hers. Between the hoots and hollers of the audience and the fuzzy background noise, Charly was unable to hear anything but the words breathed in her ear.

"You know how much I love you, don't you?"

Her body shook with anticipation and love, as well as a touch of fear, as she nodded against his cheek.

***

Charly thanked the babysitter then closed and locked the door behind her. After setting the alarm and turning out the lights, she wandered down the hall to check on her children. Bree and Chloe slept in the same room. They had been born within minutes of one another, but that's where their "twinness" ended. Breanna insisted upon nightgowns—her sister, only pajamas. Chloe slept sprawled out, covers askew—her sister, perfectly curled to one side, the linens exactly where they'd been tucked in. Charly shook her head. Chloe was her father's daughter, and Bree hers, each twin perfectly mirroring one parent

Heading to the master bedroom, she left the girls' bedroom door ajar, as she always did. She heard the shower running. *The kids are asleep...maybe we can get away with this!* Quickly, she turned down the bed.

Intimacy had seemed hit and miss as of late. She was busy with her job, and he had necessary off-season workouts. She shuttled the girls to preschool and a myriad of after-school activities. When his training schedule allowed, he loved helping his dad and brothers with their ever-growing dairy operation. With the house, charity events, relatives, and both of them running themselves ragged, it'd been awhile since they had the kind of time Charly hoped they could steal together now.

She undressed as she went into the bathroom. The stunning silhouette of her husband shadowed the frosted glass of the shower stall. Cracking the door ever so slightly, her mouth watered as she watched her husband. All six foot three of him was propped up against the tile, tepid water streaming over his broad shoulders, slithering down his chest, and over his muscled abdomen. But what got her attention most was his exquisite dick, lathered and slipping through his powerful hand.

"What're you doin' baby?" she asked.

He looked up from his work, unembarrassed. "Finishing what you started with those looks at the bar."

Charly held her breath, watching him lick his lips as he eyed her body. The greedy need in his eyes tweaked a pulse between her thighs. Regrouping, she feigned total innocence, "*Moi*? I didn't do anything."

"Hmmm, on the twenty-minute ride home you had your hand in my crotch the entire time." He opened the door all the way, grabbed her hand, and pulled her into the shower with him.

He drew her to him, and she sighed in his embrace. Warm water sluiced between their bare bodies. She caressed her bare breasts against the hard muscles of his chest, while his stiffness pressed against her. She looked up into his face, and he cleared her wet hair from her forehead, tucking it behind her ears.

Pressing his lips to her forehead, he breathed, "Give me a hand, will ya?"

"Be happy to," she teased in return. Pressing against him, she used her body to direct him to the stall's tiled seat. Widening her stance, she straddled one of his knees, maneuvering in such a way that when perched upon him she'd pleasure herself as well. She took a deep breath, glancing between them. In her mind *this* part of his anatomy had as much beauty as the rest of him—well-formed, strong, and what she knew he could do with it!

She wrapped her hand around his long, thick member, moving slowly with purpose and determination. Leaning into him, grazing his cheek with hers, she said quietly, "Tell me how you want it, baby." He lifted his chin, the whiskers of his close-cropped beard prickling against her cheek, and then her neck. She forced her to move herself against his knee.

"Charly, you know *exactly* how I want it."

He grasped her bottom with strong wet hands, holding her steady as his long legs stretched out before him. She took her time sliding down the length of his leg to kneel before him. Resting her cheek on his tightly muscled thigh, she went to pleasurable work.

With one hand she continued to spiral stroke his dick, the other clutched and manipulated his ample sac. She smiled, knowing she petted him just the right way. *Tell me, Andy, tell me I'm the only one who's done you like this—the* right *way. You always used to tell me that.* As she slipped her hand farther under him, kneading the sensitive area between his balls and anus, he shivered and a sharp groan left him.

Charly rose up, rubbing her face against Andy's tight chest. *Got you where I want you.* When she licked and nibbled on his nipple, he hissed and forced his cock more severely into her grasp. "I need a squirt, Andy."

Panting he returned, "Oh, I'm sure you're going to get one."

"Mmm, I know, but I'm talking about soap."

Like a man without energy, he reached for shower gel, squeezing a good amount onto his dick and into her hand.

She stroked him faster with one hand and moved the other with more precision. His body stiffened under her as she gently she prodded at his hole.

"Dear shit, Charly!"

"Like that, huh?" He trembled in response.

As she manipulated her husband the way she knew he adored, her mind raced with thoughts. Insecurities took center stage in her head. After all the years they'd been together she still wanted to hear how much he needed her, wanted her, that no matter what city or trade or trouble came between them, that nothing would ever truly divide what they shared. *C'mon Andy, help a girl out—tell me about the first time I ever did this to you.* As she eased her middle finger into his crack, her palm pressed against his tightening balls. Peeking up at him, she smiled. He rested his head back into the tile, eyes closed. He touched her shoulder with one hand, while his other held tight to the shower seat. She loved it when he slipped into sexual nirvana, and nothing made her happier than knowing *she* was taking him there. *If only you'd* tell *me that.*

"You think anyone on your 'list' would do this?" Of course, the "list" she referred to is the one every couple has. Five completely unattainable fucks. But if one of them *happened* to show up at the front door, one spouse would grant a pass long enough to allow the other's fantasy to be fulfilled with that actor, model, or musician.

"Do what?" he groaned.

She continued working him, inside and out. She rose up the best she could, leaning into him, requesting his attention. "You know"—she gave him a good solid poke, which sent him into a fit of moans and shivers—"uh, *finger* you." She watched as he fluttered his eyes, his mouth tweaking into a little grin.

"Well?"

"Maybe Cache, yeah, Treena Cache definitely."

With his eyes closed, he couldn't see her reaction of disgust at her husband's choice. *Really that Carrie Underwood-Miranda Lambert wannabe whore?* "But since she's not here...."

Despite her somewhat wild college time in Europe, her list of lovers still could be tallied on one hand. Yet, no other had ever allowed her to do what she did now with her husband. Andy telegraphed his readiness with a sigh and relaxing of his lower body. With help of the shower gel and his willingness, she dipped two middle fingers inside him.

His body suddenly alive, he writhed, his ass fucking her one hand, his dick screwing the other.

"Deeper, Charly, deeper!"

Although he could be a long fuck, she felt him nearing his breaking point. When she scissored her fingers inside him, fingertips feathering his prostate, he erupted.

Kneeling before him, she winced, trapped as his sphincter strangled her fingers. That minor discomfort was placated by her joy and arousal as streams of cum spewed into her other hand.

A resounding, "Fuck me!" echoed off the tile.

He caressed her head, and she released him. Climbing into his lap, she reveled in his strength and warmth. She rested her head on his shoulder and sighed when brought her into his embrace. She felt his heart pounding against her chest.

They sat, quiet, recovering, until she patted him, requesting release. Turning off the shower, she popped open the door. Clouds of steam streamed into the cooler air of the bathroom. Before she could snag a towel, Andy did, tossing it over his shoulder. She stifled a surprised squeak when he scooped her into his strong arms.

He carried her into the bedroom and placed her back on her feet at the edge of their large bed. Charly closed her eyes, swimming in the warmth of her husband and his caring caresses as he dried her with the bath sheet. When she opened her eyes, he smiled at her, moving in for a kiss. His kiss and the gentle insistence of his body directed her to the mattress.

His hand ventured between her legs. "Mmm...still wet from the shower."

When he slipped two strong fingers into her, she arched her back, wanting but unable to breathe his name, her mouth too occupied by his talented tongue. She relished his long, masterful kisses, his strong heft above her. "Andy," she pleaded. His mouth left hers, and he withdrew his fingers. He slipped down the length of her body, licking and nipping the entire way. He knelt on the carpeted floor. She closed her eyes and let him work his incredible oral magic.

Andy grazed her thighs, his callused hands encouraging them apart. She bristled at the cooler air of the bedroom and the prickles of whiskers on her mound. He opened her with loving fingers, suckling her labia, his hot insistent tongue swirling over her clit and dipping into her hole.

She'd never felt 'safe enough' with anyone but him to allow this type of intimacy. "Andy," she moaned. She touched his hair and he stopped for a moment, looking up at her. "Please tell me you're ready again."

His beautiful grin turned her to jelly every time. He climbed back on the bed, his heft shadowing over her, his again-stiff cock teasing her leg.

He nuzzled her ear. "You think I can pound a boy into you this time?"

In all her life, nothing made her feel as important, as wanted, as cherished, as these incredibly deep, close, loving moments with her husband and friend. But she couldn't silence the thoughts in her brain, even at this moment. *It doesn't matter what team he's going to, everything will be all right, he'll be home a couple times this summer....* She forced the thoughts aside, focusing on moving beneath her husband, finding a better angle for her pleasure. "Baby, yes!"

"Right there, honey? Oh yeah, right fucking there!"

She moaned in near-ecstasy as her husband banged her. *Just a little harder....*

Through their collective panting, she heard a plaintive whine. "Mommy."

"Andy," she whispered, grabbing his hips, trying to still his fervor as her motherly hearing strained.

"Mommy?" The sleepy voice broke slightly, on the verge of tears. Their daughter, concerned and confused.

"Shit." He held up, flung the linens over the both of them, and slowly withdrew.

Turning her face into a pillow, she tried to hide her irritation due to their coitus interruptus. "Darn it!"

As Andy rolled off her, she grabbed the sheets, assuring they were both covered. *How is he going to explain this?*

He sat up and took a breath. "What is it, Bree-baby?" he said, his voice gravelly with the remainder of sexual excitement.

"I sleep in your bed, Daddy."

He answered gently. "You're a big girl, Bree. You need to sleep in your own bed."

"No...your bed."

"Breanna."

"Mommy." A small yodel came from the doorway. Chloe stood there, smiling, holding up wet pajama bottoms. "I peed."

Slipping out the other side of the bed, Charly grabbed a nearby T-shirt and put it on. Flushed with near-orgasm and frustrated due to the lack of one, she checked herself.

"Which one do you want?" Andy asked, chuckling. His back to his family, he slipped out of bed and went hunting for cover. He returned in short order wearing long-line briefs.

"That didn't last long."

"Children make you go *soft*, fast, in so many ways." Leaning over, he kissed her cheek.

"As usual. I guess I'll take that as an apology and a rain check." The words left her mouth with more irritation than she intended. She watched as he easily lifted Bree up into their bed. She did her best to hide her disappointment. She took Chloe's hand. "C'mon, baby. Mommy'll clean you up."

Ten minutes later, two little girls were both dry and asleep. And, as Breanna insisted, in their parents' bed. Charly rested her head against her husband's. "Sorry, hon."

"About what?"

She looked around the bed. "The interruption. My irritation. Too little of *you know what* these days, and then...."

"Hey." His warm fingertip lifted her chin. "I love you." Kissing her gently, he promised, "There's always tomorrow." He winked at her in the darkened room. "And I'll make sure you get off like you've never gotten off before." He stopped for a moment, cuddling a daughter. "Anyway, this is *almost* as good."

"I guess we need to put a lock on that door."

"What for? That would ruin all the excitement!"

Quietly, as to not wake their girls, they laughed together.

The thoughts that had darted to the front of her brain earlier in the evening, returned. A question spilled from her mouth before she had any chance to stop it. "So, this trade," she began.

"Yes, Charlotte."

No, not my given first name, this is not going to be good. "You know, don't you?"

"I didn't want to upset, you Char."

So you were keeping me in the dark! "Just tell me, Andy."

"New...."

"No...." With the utterance of that one word, she *knew*. A city she loathed, a metropolis that had emotionally chewed her up and spit her out. She hadn't been to The City in more than a decade, and it would take some doing to get her to return.

"...York, the Bronx."

Swallowing hard, she blocked the tears. A defeated, disgusted sigh left her. "No, Andy, not New York, not the Titans." Cuddling Chloe closer, she turned her face from her husband and cried herself to sleep.

Chapter Three

Two weeks later, the spring baseball rituals began. As much as she hated it, still Charly put on a happy face. If this were any other year, the girls would've been outfitted in little Milwaukee Breakers shirts, but mentally holding her nose, she honored her husband by dressing them in tiny Titans jerseys. They sat atop their father's carry-on at the front door.

Charly watched as he squatted in front of them.

"Daddy's going to miss you." He clutched them tightly, smooching them wetly on the cheeks.

"Daddy going to *Forida*," Bree mentioned.

"*Florida,* baby."

"For what," he asked.

"Springtime training."

"Close enough, baby," he whispered to Bree.

"We come see you, Daddy," Chloe told him.

"That's right. Mommy will bring you." Hugging them again, he said his good-byes.

When he rose to meet Charly, there were tears in his eyes.

"What, Andy?"

Taking her into his arms and holding her tightly, he whispered, "This gets harder all the time."

Knowing that, she didn't let on how much his leaving affected her as well, especially since in Florida, there'd be no familiar faces to hang with, no women who understood her and she them. She'd be with strangers. "But, it's what you do, honey." She hugged him in return, kissing his cheek. "We'll see you in a week or two." His hold tightened about her.

His voice quiet, nearly apologetic, he confessed, "I'm sorry we haven't had a chance to 'get busy' lately, Charly. You know how

20

much I'm going to miss that." He kissed her ear, his voice even more quiet, secretive, "I'll ask Mom to come to Florida with you. We can get a little alone time then." His took her face in his hands and brought his lips to hers for a long, deep, gotta-make-it-last kiss.

When the car service driver rang the doorbell, a not so pretty chapter in their lives began.

***

"*Mon amour,* have you seen this?" Josef, waved *New York Magazine* at Paul. The gallery always had a collection of arts-centric publications from major metropolitan areas.

"Haven't gotten to that one, babe, too busy concentrating on *Oostburg Today*," he joked with his boyfriend. Leaning back, his head rested in Josef's midsection as he reached around to show him the publication. He sighed, happy and complete. *I would have spent ten times what I did for Madame Eve's help!*

"But you need to see this." Josef dropped the open publication on the table in front of him, resting his chin on his lover's shoulder. In the middle of the photo, Andy Knox and his new teammate, Blake Huntington, were dressed to the nines. The full page ad had the newest Titans smothered in nearly bare bodies and breasts. "I don't think any of those mammaries are connected to his lovely wife."

"I know I'm late—again," came a happy call from the front of the gallery. "I had to drop off the girls."

The two men looked up, as Charly walked in. They tried *not* to appear in "the know."

"Boys," she mentioned, dropping a purse, hanging a coat. "What's going on?"

Paul clandestinely slid the pages under the desktop blotter. He caught her raising a questioning eye brow.

"Out with it. What's gonna piss me off on this fine Friday morning?"

"Oh, nuthin', darling."

She put out her hand like only a mother can. With nothing more than her palm and her grimace, she insisted the boys turn over whatever it was they were hiding. With a glance at Josef, Paul handed over the incriminating paper and watched as Charly's usually happy appearance began to slide—concern, sadness, and anger all played in her eyes, her mouth, and her bearing.

"I hate that he's clean-shaven."

That's odd. He let the statement hang in the air, not sure what it meant or what it might convey.

No one moved for what seemed a very long minute. Then, Paul had to dodge the offending publication being flung back to his desk.

Charly turned and stormed back out into the brisk April air.

***

"Charly, I don't know what you're talking about." Andy nodded hello to teammate Blake Huntington, then wandered to the pool area of the Miami hotel where the players were slowly trickling in for breakfast.

"Not even three weeks into the regular season and I'm looking at shit like this?"

Something was *seriously* wrong. Rarely did his wife use expletives *and* not sound relatively sane. "Take a breath, honey, take a breath." He said the words calmly and with the most respect and care. Hearing Charly cry on the other end of the phone pained his heart. "Baby, what is it?"

Acrid sarcasm shot through the phone. "Oh nothing—just women slathering their tits all over you and that man whore, Huntington, in *New York Magazine*."

Shaking his head, confused, Andy had no idea what would propel his wife into such a state. "Listen to me, baby, *nothing is* going on...nothing." Those were words he had used in the past, before they were married, *knowing* at the time they were untrue. Back then, Charly had easily seen through the "nothing's going on" statement. He'd issued it while he was standing in the doorway of a hotel room with a drunk, naked woman behind him. Compared to then, nothing *was* going on. "It was a photo shoot, kind of 'dressing the new guys like they belong in Manhattan' kind of thing."

Silence. She wasn't buying it.

"How many years have we done this?" Andy continued. "Spring training, road games, away from each other for weeks at a time? We both knew what we were signing up for. But, I didn't sign anything that stated when away from you I'd be unfaithful in *any* way. To the contrary, honey, you know that."

More silence.

"I know it's different this time. During home games, I'm not *at home.* It's not Milwaukee, it's New York City. It's not quiet, it's loud. It's not happily blue collar, it's the Waldorf Astoria and Wall Street. Haven't you always told me to enjoy every place I'm in? I had no idea about the models."

Cricket, cricket.

"But you shaved."

Shaving must equate to infidelity. C'mon, baby, what's going on in your head?

"You know the rules. New team, no facial hair. I shave before every game, darlin'."

"I don't like it."

His thoughts turned R-rated, "I don't either, 'cause I know how my whiskers tickle your...."

He nearly dropped the phone when her voice came bellowing through it. "I don't know what you're finding so amusing, Andrew Ryan Patrick Knox!"

Oh, crap—my entire given name, she's really *pissed.* "Listen, hon, next weekend we play Chicago. I can spend a couple nights at home."

Irrational words blasted through the phone. "*Home?* Wouldn't that be your Central Park apartment?"

"Charly! Knock it off!" *Christ, woman, get a fucking grip!* He strolled as far from any co-workers and loitering fans as he could. No one needed to know his personal business. As diligently as he tried, he couldn't stop his voice from taking a curt tone. "What *is* the matter with you? I don't know what the *fuck* you *think* I'm doing out here, but whatever it *is*, lose the fucking thought!"

"Don't *even* talk to me like."

Dammit, I hate it when I yell at you, but... "Shut up and listen! If you're going to concern yourself with something you *know* I will never do, then I have *every fucking right* to use this tone of voice." He stopped, trying to calm himself, hoping he could calm her. Glancing about, he hoped no one had overheard his confused anger. Quietly, he continued, still hearing her sniffle so many miles away. "I love you, baby. I *am not* 'that guy.' I love you and the girls with everything I am. I don't like being away any more than you do, but we both know *this* is what I do. No matter where I am, my heart and home are with you, honey."

He let her be for a moment, allowing his words sink in. "I'm sorry, hon, that I'm here and you're there. I know this season is different from years past. And, I'm very sorry"—he checked his surroundings, hoping for no accidental eavesdroppers, and lowered his voice—"that we didn't get around to...*you know*...my last night home."

The expression of missed intimacy never found its mark. He'd hoped the words would soften her, making her realize her importance, even if they weren't physically together.

A loud sniffle came through the receiver. "I just feel so distant from you, Andy, and I don't mean miles. Like I'm tucked in the back of your mind, not the front of it, and I'm afraid you're going to forget me there."

He knew exactly what she implied. Imagining her beautiful face, saddened by his actions, hurt him beyond measure. There would *never* be a way for him to make amends for his past misdeeds.

***

They were hunkered down at "their" table, at "their" bar. Although a leisurely five minute stroll from the gallery in the touristy Old World Third Street neighborhood of downtown Milwaukee, this wasn't a tourist attraction. It was a plain old neighborhood tavern, like any you'd find on every corner of every large or small Wisconsin town.

Charly put her face in her hands, disgusted. Casey stroked her back, silently trying to convey to his friend's wife everything would be all right. Casey Rupp, the former ballplayer, now with a "doctor" in front of his first name, was Andy's longtime friend and had been the best man at their wedding. He happened to be in town consulting on some physical training for a couple of the Milwaukee-area college teams. The two spoke quietly while they waited for Paul.

"It's different this time, Casey. I'm accustomed to him being home half the summer. We're just so...um...disconnected, like being a couple is so hit and miss."

"You knew a trade someday would be a possibility, there aren't many career-franchise players anymore. You *must* trust him. You know there's no reason not to."

She straightened in her seat. Taking a deep breath she turned to her friend, looking straight into his eyes. "I don't know, this morning he actually *yelled* at me on the phone."

"C'mon, Charly."

"I'm not blind, I'm not stupid. He's not *here*, so who knows what he's doing?"

"Maybe he's in a museum trying to understand what you and Paul inherently *know*. Maybe he's shopping for something special for you and the girls. Maybe he's working out or most likely, sitting in his hotel room missing *you*."

"And, maybe he's not. The whole trade, how it happened, Andy being okay with it, the situation seemed *wrong*, Casey. Then that photo spread in *New York Magazine*." She dug into her voluminous bag and yanked out the offending photo, tossing it on the table in front of Casey.

"Oh shit." *Damn, what the fuck was he thinking? Say no to the front office media machine, bud!*

"Yes, oh shit." She paused for a moment, lost. "I don't know what to do." She tossed back what was left of her second brandy old-fashioned and waved at the barkeep for another.

Witnessing the velocity of her slamming her drink, Casey knew there was *nothing* he could say to get his old friend out of the dog house with his wife in her current state.

At the same time, he *could* empathize with her, being away from the one he loved. There'd never been much of a discussion with his fiancée, Abby, but if two people were in love and committed, what *was* there to discuss? Trust was a given and inherent. *Wasn't it?* He could all but see his logical fiancée raising her eyebrows at his truly masculine way of thought. Still he had to ask, "Have you told him how you feel?"

"Really, Casey? You're a man. You know how men react when a woman 'tells you how she feels.' Puh-leeze. I can see his brown eyes rolling up into his head, and he's thinking, *What fucking hormone train did she get on this morning?* And then a bunch of nodding and uh huhs, and we get nowhere."

"I think you're being a bit harsh, he's not that way."

Her acidic tone bordered on straight-up bitchy. "How do you know? You're not married, and you're certainly not married to him." She snatched her purse from the table.

"Where are you going?"

"To pee and cry. Is that all right?"

Casey just nodded. He vowed he'd never become that complacent with his relationship. Pulling his phone from his pocket, he opened a text to his fiancée. *Hello, baby. Will try to call you later. Out right now with Andy's wife. She's having some separation anxiety – long story.*

A ping replied a moment later, *Hi! As much as I miss you, if she needs your help, you're there. Need to meet them both sometime. I think it's ridiculous I'm getting better at texting, but my bro says I'm a natural because of my good hands. LOL.*

Casey smiled. He knew Abby loathed texting. *Good,* strong hands. *And I miss them right now.*

Stop! Love you, babe, but gotta run, just sat for 5 mins. Got a kid I have to keep my eye on. Pray for no amputation.

Will do, hon. Good luck with the kid. Kissing you in my mind. Nite.

Love you, Casey. See you tomorrow my hot fiancé!

He shook his head thinking about Dr. Abigail Lewis, his fiancée, eight years his senior. He wondered what he'd seen in dating women his own age or younger. He'd had second thoughts about using a dating service, but Madame Eve and her 1Night Stand had fulfilled his every wish in a woman, and before the year ended, he'd be married to that woman.

Seeing Paul wander in the bar, Casey waved him over. He had to hold back a slight snicker watching the art dealer precisely remove his Yves Saint Laurent leather motocross jacket. Casey was sure this man had *never* been on a bike, much less a motocross cycle or crotch-rocket.

"Mr. Rupp," the gallery owner put out his hand. "How wonderful to see you again!" He sat, smiling. "I see Charly took the liberty to order me a...."

"I did, Belvedere and tonic," Casey replied, shaking Paul's hand. He *swore* the man winked at him and squeezed tighter.

Releasing him and waving his hand a little too lightly for Casey's taste, he touched the former ballplayer on the wrist. "You remembered! Such a kind man you are, Casimir."

And, he remembers my given name. I am in such *trouble here!* "It's the least I can do for the man watching over my best friend's wife."

Paul leaned forward, a bit too close for Casey's liking, but he didn't flinch. "She's a mess, isn't she?"

"I've never seen her like this, and I've known her probably as long as you have. She's usually so with it, and takes Andy being away in stride."

"She hates New York, you know," he mentioned, sipping. "She had a bad experience there when she was in art school. She doesn't talk about it much."

"She never mentioned anything to me, but it always struck me as odd that she never would *go* to New York when Andy would play there."

"They broke up there," Paul whispered.

"Seriously?" Casey'd never heard that story.

"It was before they were engaged. He got caught up in some I'm-a-young-hot-studly-baseball-player nightlife, got drunk, forgot all about meeting up with her—until she found him in his hotel room...."

Casey watched as the man arched his perfectly trimmed eyebrows. "He didn't."

"That's never been made clear, but it broke her heart—broke *his*, too." Quickly he touched his index finger to his lips and cocked his head toward the back of the bar, "Shh!"

"Pauly!" Both men rose, and Charly pecked her boss's cheek.

He slid over, putting his arm about her. "Have I told you, Casey, this woman makes more money than a fresh, tight-pussied whore walking through Times' Square during Fleet Week?"

"Stop it, Paul," she nudged.

"But it's true, honey." He leaned forward to mask a huge financial secret. "She sold three million dollars' worth of art in the past month and a half."

"Well, at least I'm good at *something*," she sighed.

Casey watched, concerned, as she took a long sip of her old-fashioned, and then "tasted" half of Paul's vodka tonic.

He took the glass from her, but not before she drank the remainder of it. "Self-pity is not good color on you, honey. Cut this shit out."

"Leave me alone, you old queen. How could you possibly understand."

Neither man had ever heard this caustic, accusatory, and plain mean tone before. It spewed from her lovely mouth in a much more acerbic manner than the usual playful, sarcastic banter between employer and employee at the gallery. Paul was a good man, with an amazing work ethic, kind, generous, and forgiving, but even Casey wouldn't tolerate name calling, especially when Paul was Charly's employer, confidant, and good friend. Her tone and self-wallowing belied more than just missing her husband.

With good reason, Paul snapped. "Listen here, you smart-mouthed, untrusting little twat. If anyone would know what the fuck you're going through, it's *me, your friend.* Your gay-as-the-day-is-long confidant whose man isn't nearby all the time either."

Casey watched as the woman put up a hand in apology and to interject, but Paul cut her off.

"Sure Josef's here *now,* but like your Andy, he'll be gone at the end of the week. To where? A tropical garden *ripe* with opportunities to fall off the fidelity wagon. So, don't talk to me about how I couldn't *possibly* know what you're going through. I might not have a ring on my finger, and haven't spit out two gorgeous little girls, but *love and trust,* honey, is just that, whether it's two dicks, or a dick and slit, *love and trust...*either you believe it, ascribe to it, or you don't. And for some reason, right now, you're not."

Even Casey had to take breath after that monologue, which, regardless of its sincere honesty, obviously didn't have the effect Paul had hoped.

Her face in her hands, she leaned forward, resting on the tabletop, her body shaking with sobs.

Both men leaned in, ready to comfort, but at the same time anxious get to the bottom of the destructive behavior. "What the hell is wrong with you, Charly?" Casey insisted.

"You have *no* idea." Tears streaked her pretty face. She snatched her purse and coat from the booth seat and started for the door.

"Go, go." Paul waved at Casey.

***

Charly rested her head against the cool glass of her car window. The seat beneath her felt strange, like she didn't quite fit in it.

"You all right, Charly?" Casey asked.

She nodded, her head making the tiniest of squeaking noises against the window. *Now I know why this feels so odd! I'm never a passenger in my own car.*

Closing her eyes, she focused on taking a slow, deep breath. Doing so scattered the vertigo caused by the blacktop of I-43 flying by below her.

"We need to get you something to eat. Drive through?"

She shot down the idea with a quick shake of her head. *Bad idea. Now the whole car is spinning.* Again closing her eyes, she embraced the disequilibrium. *Maybe centrifugal force will fling all these bullshit thoughts from my head!*

A few minutes later, the car slowed. Raising her head, Charly saw her garage door in front of her.

"Your button doesn't work, Char."

"It's not programmed. Andy was supposed to take care of it before he...." *Before he fucking left for New York!* "And, I must've left the spare opener in the other car."

"C'mon." Casey put out his hand, to help her from the vehicle.

Damn, I didn't even notice he got out. "I'm perfectly capable of getting out of my car, Casey. Geez." Waving him off, she insisted her body find balance and focus. She kept her hand on her car as she made her way around the vehicle to the garage keypad. "If you would've let me drive home, I wouldn't have to break into my own house." She poked at the numbers.

"No way that was going to happen! Not with all the liquor you put away today."

Her number poking turned to number pounding. "What the hell is the code!"

"Why don't we just go around to the front door?" Casey asked.

Without bashing her finger against another digit, the garage door started going up.

A young woman's voice came from inside the garage. "Mrs. Knox? Charly?"

"Kristen! It's me. Thanks for opening up."

"Well, three bad tries and the alarm peeps. Thought I better check."

Charly saw the babysitter give a concerned look to the stranger hitting the garage door Close button. "He's an old friend. He drove me home." She put her hand to her mouth, holding back a hiccup. "Been one of those days."

"Uh, looks like it. You want me to stay, I'll call my mom."

"Could you?"

"Sure."

She put her arm about the girl's shoulders. "The little sister I never had."

Turning her toward Casey, she introduced them. "Kristen, if I hadn't married Andy, this guy would be the father of my children. Kristen, Casey. Casey, Kristen. I gotta pee." She wandered into the house, her babysitter and guest following behind.

***

Charly weaved her way back into the kitchen and plopped herself at the table next to Casey. "My two angels are asleep, Kristen is staying the night, and here we are." She stopped for a moment, looking at her friend. "What?"

He shrugged, "Nothin'."

"Nothin' never means nothin' coming from a man's mouth."

Casey snickered and shook his head.

"You're laughing at me because I'm a little tipsy, right?"

"No, Charly, I think you're flat out hammered, and if you had driven home, you never would have made it."

She leaned against him. "Then it's a good thing you're in town." She rose from the table and headed toward the refrigerator. "Unlike some people," she mumbled.

"What did you say?"

She turned to him, holding a bottle of wine she'd taken from the fridge. Straightening her posture, she lifted her chin and enunciated as clearly as possible, considering the alcohol-induced slur. "Un. Like. Some. People."

"That's Andy's job, Charly, you know that."

She placed the bottle and a corkscrew in front of him.

"You're kidding, right? You're actually going to drink some *more?*"

"Hey, I'm home, you're here, I have an overnight babysitter. What difference does it make?" She felt his warm hand around her arm, gently bringing her back into her seat. "Just open it, Case."

"What's wrong with you, Charly?" he asked, starting on the cork. "You have the world by the ass, and you're unhappy."

"I'm not unhappy, just concerned and lonely." Casey slid a glass in front of her. "Thank you." She held hers up to him. "To good friends who listen."

They clinked and drank.

Charly took her time returning her glass to the table. She stared into the pale liquid and sighed. Her concentrated interest broke when a box of bear-shaped graham crackers slid into her view.

"I hate seeing you like this."

"Like what, drunk?"

"No, sad, wallowing. Unsure, I guess. It's not like you."

"You don't know me very well then, Casey." She felt a choke forming in her throat. *I am not going to fucking cry.* She pulled a paper napkin from the holder on the table and hid her face in it.

"Then tell me, kid, what the hell is going on?"

She wiped her face and turned to her friend. Tears ran down her cheeks and she let them. "I'm lonely, Casey. I know that's part of the 'deal' in this profession, but now Andy is gone the *entire* season, not eight-one games. Bree and Chloe don't understand why he's not home. And when he is home, we're so hit and miss."

"What do you mean?"

"What I mean, we seem like strangers to one another. I couldn't get to spring training with the girls—the flu 'round robin' at their preschool." She stopped for a sip of wine and to collect her thoughts. "We talk on the phone and it's like his mind is constantly elsewhere, preoccupied. He's not himself. And," she continued quietly, "we haven't done our 'marital duty' since before spring training. Yes, add it up...three months plus." Her face reddened with the admission.

"There's more to life than that."

"Not when you're trying to have another baby." She sighed, resigned, "Right now, there's no time for us, he's in New York, running with a completely different crowd, one I don't fit in. He's a different person now that he's with the Titans."

"Changing a uniform doesn't change the person, Charly."

"The *hell* it doesn't! He goes to New York, and the next thing I know, he's changed his looks, his clothes, and has naked women draped all over him! We both know how many marriages went south after a trade to that organization and that city."

"But you went to art school there."

"One semester, then I *had* to leave. I went to Florence for almost a year."

"Why did you *have* to leave?"

"Does it matter what happened how many years ago?"

"If it has some bearing on—"

"I'm afraid I'm losing him, Case. This has never been so hard. Sometimes I wonder if he even loves me."

She felt the alcohol and gravity of her words take over. Leaning into Casey, she let the sobs come. Anger, concern, sadness all left her as she wept. The close hold of a dear friend helped to stabilize her condition, leaving her with one last emotion—spite.

What happened years ago consumed her. Not a vengeful person, she'd never found a way, or actually *wanted* to get back at Andy. Well, not until now, when alcohol-fueled irritation emboldened her. She snaked her arms about his neck and shoulders, hoping for a meaningful embrace, one she could hold on to in her darkest moments—a memory of a hug she could revisit when she needed it most, when she felt most forgotten and unloved.

"It's all right, Charly."

She allowed herself the wallowing. Crying into his shoulder, she reveled in his strong arms. When she hid her face in the curve of his neck, the scratch of his short-cut auburn whiskers against her skin forced her emotions in another direction.

Charly took a deep breath. Casey's spicy scent calmed her tears, replacing any sadness with a stirring she *only* felt in very quiet intense moments with her husband. The devil on her one shoulder flipped its middle finger at the angel on the other. She rubbed her face on his skin, taking a moment to kiss his neck in a way any man would understand. "I always thought you were so hot, Casey."

"Stop."

He clutched her upper arms and returned her to an upright sitting position. His large hands surrounded hers, sending a clear message that he was only willing to allow her so much physical comfort.

Charly felt the red of embarrassment flooding up her neck.

"We've been friends forever. I've known you nearly as long as I've known Andy. I know you hurt right now, but doing something rash, like making a move on me or *anyone* else, is, number one—not you, and number two—would only cause you *and* him more hurt."

Unable to look him in the eye, she stared at her hands, slowly turning the diamonds and platinum on her left ring finger.

"What is going on with you two, Charly?"

They were saved by her phone rumbling against the tabletop. She reached forward, looked at it, frowned, the slid the device toward him. "Why don't *you* ask *him*."

***

Andy propped himself up against the headboard, getting comfortable. Holding his phone to his ear, he listened to the connection ring and ring. "C'mon, Charly, pick up." While waiting for an answer, he tried to determine what city he was in. It'd been a long flight and, upon arrival, he remembered landing, checking in and that was about it. The rest of the information lost to a nap that had sneaked up on him.

"Hello, Andy."

"Uh, hello?" *My wife's voice has definitely changed.*

"Andy, it's Casey."

"Hey Case! Shit, I'm must've misdialed. I just woke up."

"Where are you?"

"I have no fucking idea," he chuckled. "Seattle, I think."

"Well, you didn't misdial. I'm in Milwaukee."

"And you're answering my wife's phone, why?"

"And it's nice to hear your voice, too!" The friends laughed together. "We were out for drinks with Paul. She had a few, plus a few more, and one on top of that. I didn't want her getting snagged by the Milwaukee cops, and you know how serious the Ozaukee County deputies are."

"That's concerning."

"She's checking on the girls."

"So, a little on the hammered side?"

"Uh, let's just say, her natural gait right now is weaving and bobbing."

Andy heard Casey's awkward chuckle.

After a moment, his friend asked, "What's going on with you two? There's obviously *something* wrong."

"New York is what happened. She hates the idea home games aren't at home any longer. With good reason."

"What reason?"

The connection remained quiet for some time. "I cheated on her, man," he finally whispered.

Chapter Four

"You. Did. What?"

Andy heard the disgust in Casey's tone. It hurt that one of his oldest and dearest friends would probably be good and pissed after this phone conversation. "It happened before we were engaged."

"That's not an excuse."

Andy reached for a framed photo which visited every city with him. Three beautiful females smiled back at him from the frame— Charly, Breanna, and Chloe. "You're right, it's not."

"Is this why your wife is in such a state?"

"Probably. This all happened years ago in New York."

For some time, silence colored the connection between the two men, until Andy explained. "It was my first stint with the Breakers, first season with them. I was in New York for the league championship, two games there. Charly and I spent my off time together. Well, until we won the second game. Ran into someone I used to know, got a little fucked up, and forgot to meet her for dinner. She came looking for me—and found me in my hotel room."

"Then what happened?"

"I mean, we were *seeing* one another, but there was never any real discussion about it being an exclusive relationship at the time and...."

"If you were seeing her often and sleeping with her, in *her* mind, it was an exclusive relationship."

"I know that now. But then, I wasn't sure...and I fucked it up. It's *my* fault she left art school in New York. It's *my* fault she hates the city. *Of course,* I want to preserve the great thing I have. I don't want to fuck up again, but we're on different pages when it comes to this trade. She's not thrilled, but agreed that if I wanted to keep playing, it's what I—what *we*—had to do. And you know the money's pretty damn good. But, this being away, for more than the normal extended periods of time, keeps her worked up, tosses her back to the time I *did* fuck up."

"You need to fix this, Knox and—"

"You think I don't want to?" he interrupted. "I can only say nothing's going on so much. If she's not going to believe me, what can I do?"

"Saying no to that magazine photo shoot for starters. I love ya, brother, but you had to know something like that would bother her."

"I didn't know a thing about the models—"

"You could have avoided this entire situation."

"I know, but I didn't. What's done is done. To be honest, Rupp, I don't know *what* to do about it."

"Do you love her?"

"*Of course*, I do." The thought hung for a moment, then Andy admitted, "More than she'll ever know or could imagine. I mean, this isn't like what happened with her parents."

"What happened with her folks?"

"Ah, shit, Casey. Her dad was pretty obvious about his infidelities, and then he dumped her mom when she was ill, and left them with pretty much nothing."

"No wonder she's so fucking upset, Knox. That shit doesn't go away, no matter how intelligent and rational Charly is."

Andy said nothing. No words could fix what he had broken years ago. As much as he knew Charly had done her best to put her familial past behind her and become a well-adjusted adult, Andy knew the scar of that particular hurt never *completely* healed.

"I have an idea."

"I'll take any help at this moment, Rupp."

"I'm gonna text you from *my* phone. Don't ask any questions, just follow the instructions and this will all work out."

"You're scaring the shit out of me, Casey. What is this?"

"Trust me, Knox. I'm a doctor, remember?"

***

Charly woke up with tears streaming down her face and a clanging headache. When she found Casey making the twins and Kristen breakfast, she turned right around, went back to her bedroom, and cried even more. *Nothing happened. If it had, the babysitter still wouldn't be here.* Friday in its entirety came flooding back and sadness regarding her martial situation draped a wet blanket over Saturday.

After breakfast, Charly slipped Kristen two one hundred dollar bills and sent her home.

"Are you sure you're going to be all right?" Casey asked. He stood at the front door and slipped on his Adidas jacket.

She could barely look him in the eye, still embarrassed by last night's disgusting attempt at finding some kind, *any kind,* of affection and validation. "I will."

"Charly."

He took her into his brotherly embrace. She sucked down any inkling of a sniffle.

"When I say trust me, you'll just have to. *I'm* telling you, nothing's going on with Andy, and everything will be all right."

Nodding into his broad chest, if she didn't believe him, she tried to at least appear to. "Thanks, Casey. Thanks for looking out for me."

"Anytime. I'm headed back to Ann Arbor, but call me later if you want."

"A consult at the University of Michigan?"

"Uh, no." He gave her a wink. "My fiancée."

With that information, I'm officially even more pathetic, considering my lame move last night. Apple doesn't fall far from the tree—I'm turning into a cheater just like my dad was. "Well, um," she tripped over her own thoughts, "...congratulations. I'm sure she's wonderful." *Like I used to be to my husband.*

"Snagged myself a doctor. An older woman, too." He winked.

"Casey, I'm, uh, sorry about my behavior last night—"

He cut her off. "Stop, now, okay?" he said quietly.

She closed her eyes as he placed a comforting kiss on her forehead.

"Nothing happened, chalk it up to a combination of old-fashioneds, vodka tonics, and chardonnay."

"I appreciate your levity, Casey."

"Anytime. Take care of yourself. I mean it." He squeezed her.

A brisk April breeze blew in as he left. She had no idea what she was going to do with herself and the tormenting thoughts she couldn't oust from her mind.

***

Feigning illness, Charly called her mother-in-law and asked if she'd take the girls for the remainder of the day. Then she went back to bed, hating herself for being a willing participant in her own pity party. Still, with all that had transpired over the past day or so, she felt she deserved it.

A tiny ping caught her attention. Rolling over, she took her phone from the night stand; it reminded her about five missed calls, three texts, and two voice mails.

She listened to a voicemail from Paul first. "You better be out of bed and dressed, darling. Don't make me put you in the shower myself. I'll be over later so you can apologize." Then, in a less frivolous tone, "Love you, my dearest Charlotte. All is well, honey.

Voice mail rolled to the second message. "Hi, baby. Wanted to call and check on you. Sounds like you had a long night, and well-deserved, I imagine. I'm sorry, hon. I'm sorry I'm not there. I miss you and the girls terribly. We have an afternoon game, so call me tonight. Love you, Charly. I'll be waiting to hear your voice."

Before she had a chance to digest Andy's words, the doorbell rang.

She dragged herself to the front door, peeking through the beveled sidelight to determine whether she wanted to answer.

"I can see you, Charlotte. Open the door." Her boss rapped for good measure. "I want to hug you while I'm apologizing."

Begrudgingly, she let him in. Before she could turn away and hide her puffy, tear-laced face from him, he snagged her and pulled her in.

"Let me go, Paul."

"Not a chance, you remarkable little bitch."

He cradled her face. His hands felt so warm and soft on her skin.

"I am so sorry, my darling. My words were terribly harsh yesterday, and I didn't mean them."

She couldn't stop her tears—tears of embarrassment, regret, and worry.

"And, I know you're sincerely hating yourself too, *mon cher*. C'mon, let Pauly make you a nice mocha cappuccino, and we girls can talk."

Settled at the kitchen table, she watched him flit through the cupboards. Not only did he fire up the cappuccino machine, he found some refrigerated cinnamon rolls and put them in the oven.

"Will you marry me?" she asked, sipping his perfect brew, knowing he completely understood her sentiment.

Sitting down beside her, he touched her arm. "Honey, if I liked what you're hiding in those yoga pants, I'd be all over you!"

"Thanks." She put her face in her hands. "What am I going to do?"

"Let's dissect the trouble first, shall we? Your hot baseball boy isn't home. He's back in a place where a bunch of heartache happened. Now, you must know he's not going to go sex-rogue on you and mess up this fine family with those two adorable I-could-cover-them-with-chocolate-and-eat-them-alive little girls. So, what's going on? You're suspicious, he's *suspicious* that you're suspicious, and let me guess, it's been a little quiet in the 'nasty' department for any number of reasons. The few times he gets home, he's distracted or tired, which only causes you *more* suspicion. Charly-hon, I didn't peg you for such a suspicious little snot."

"Except—"

"Yes, except when you know I'm getting a bad deal on a piece of art."

"Thank you. Knowing I do something well is doing a great deal for my self-worth at this moment."

They were quiet, both sipping, until the beep of the oven called. He plated the rolls, slathered them in icing, and plopped a dollop of butter on top of each for good measure.

"Some caffeine, dairy, and sugar—you must feel better already." Making her another cappuccino, he continued talking. "I think I may have an idea of how to correct this situation, but I don't know if you're going to like it."

"What do you mean, '...don't know if I'm going to like it?'"

"What I mean is, you might need some outside help in all those departments that aren't getting the proper attention right now— your marriage, your relationship, and your sex life."

"I love you, my friend, but I don't know if I want to discuss my sex life with you."

"Puh-leeze, missy, like you haven't before."

"Never when I was sober."

"Well, you might have to! What about Skype sex? Ever tried that?"

She'd made sour faces in the past, but this one probably would win awards. "You're kidding, right?"

"No, hon, c'mon, wouldn't you like to see your honey's hot bod and *enormous* cock on your laptop? I mean, you both could watch each other have some fun. Josef and I do it all the time."

"No. Please, that's enough."

He waved away her disgust, chuckling. "I just wanted to see your reaction! Even after all that schooling in Paris and Florence, I'm surprised you're so...um...*prim.*"

"How prim or not-so prim I am with my husband is no one's business but his and mine, Paul."

"I know, sweetie. So, let's take it out of my hands so to speak, although I'm sure it'd be a thrill to handle Andy's—"

"Paul! Stop it!"

"Oh, darling, you so have to loosen up! *Anyway,* like I was saying, out of my hands and into those of an expert."

"I'm *not* going to a therapist."

"Oh, I would *never* suggest that, but I would suggest this." From a butter-blond leather portfolio which he had so carefully placed on a nearby kitchen chair, he extracted a beautiful parchment envelope.

"Stationery? You're suggesting I write a letter?"

He tapped her hand in playful disgust. "Just keep your pretty little silk knickers on, Charlotte." He extracted sheaves of paper from the envelope. Placing the paperwork in front of her, he said, "Read."

She scanned the pages, then stopped, handing them back. "Seriously don't want to read about your sexual activities...."

"Oh, baby doll, you are *so* missing the point."

"Which is?"

He straightened the papers precisely and slipped them back into the valise. "The point is, you need a little help. Andrew needs a little help. You both need a little help in *that* department. The woman who runs this agency—"

"From what I've read, she sounds like a modern day pimp."

"Stop that right now, young lady, and listen to me. I found the love of my life through this service. Sure, at first, it was just a hook up—and honey, let me tell you she *hooked me up!* But, somehow, Madame Eve—"

"*Madame*? She *is* a pimp!"

"I'm ignoring you, right now, and continuing my lovely story.

39

Madame Eve seems to know people's hearts and what they need. Josef and I are together because of her."

"But, wait, first and foremost, this 'Eve thing' is a hook up service."

"Well, not really, but—"

"It either is or isn't."

"Okay, it is."

"So, why would I pay good money to be hooked up with someone I'm already hooked up with?" They were both quiet for a moment, looking at each other. "But," she began, "because you love me and are always looking out for me, leave it here and I'll look it over. I *am not*, however, going to read all that personal stuff—so take those pages out."

"Why, you might get some tips that Andy would like—"

"Paul Franklin Francis Strait, stop it right now!"

"Oh, honey, you need to loosen up!" He rose and kissed the top of her head. Leaving the fancy envelope, he plucked his portfolio from the table. "See you on Monday. Do *not* be late."

"Thanks, Paulie."

"Love you, sweetheart!" he called, heading for the door.

***

Charly read three Dr. Seuss books over Facetime to the twins, including Hop on Pop. Twice. After a loving digital goodnight, she tucked them in extra snugly. She chatted with her mother-in-law before she hung up, assuring her everything was fine and that she was just having a little of a rough row with Andy away. *I know she's not buying it, but she's too classy to get in the middle of my relationship with her son.*

Twenty-four hours or so had passed since his terse words with her. *Does he get it? Does he really have any idea why I'm upset?* Maybe it was time to at least come to some agreeable way to disagree about the situation. *I'd rather have him stew, but....* With a sigh, she picked up her phone.

"Hey, honey! How ya doin'?"

He's much too chipper. "I'm all right, a little hung over."

"Nothing wrong with that, baby. A night out is good for you once in a while. I'm glad you had some time to yourself if that's what you needed."

I know what I need and I know you do too.
"Did you have a nice visit with Casey?"
"He's engaged, you know."
"What? To what, his career?"
"A doctor. An older woman, he said."

She listened as her husband went on about how it was about time for his friend. How they'd have a wedding to go to, how wonderful it was for Rupp to finally settle down. *That's all good and fine, husband, but we're not solving a thing when it comes to us.*

"We'll be in Chicago at the end of the week. Come down. Bring the girls."

She hated to cave, but he deserved to see his children, regardless how irritated *she* was with him. "I'll see what I can do."

Another fifteen minutes of innocuous chitchat, avoiding the meat of the problem, and a few awkward I love yous later, she wished her husband good night.

Turning out the light, she thought about the myriad of conversations she'd had over the past twenty-four hours. *Paul's probably right, maybe I need someone to look at this relationship from the outside. But what if that 1Night Stand place doesn't hook people up with others they know? I don't want to have an affair. I could never go through with that. And who knows how much it costs? I've gotten this far without any help, I should be able to figure this out on my own.* With a sigh, she slipped down into the sheets, wondering if her marriage would ever recover from hurt Andy had inflicted upon it.

***

The Titans arrived in Chicago too late for Andy to rent a car and spend ninety minutes zipping north to suburban Milwaukee, not with a day game looming. But he knew the three of them could join him at tomorrow's game, then they'd all go to the hotel together. He'd have two nights and portions of three days with them, which would, hopefully, be enough time to calm his wife and make amends.

Popping his head above the dugout roof, he scanned the seats searching for his girls. He found nothing, other than the usual hanger-on autograph seekers and stragglers waiting to wander the queue up and out of the stadium. *It's only a two-hour drive, Char.*

You should've been here by now
   With a sigh, he headed down the tunnel and into the clubhouse. Grabbing his phone from his locker shelf, a text message explained, *Parking lot on 94, not even to Racine.* Then, *just hitting the state line.* Finally, *Parking lot on Ohio Street. Should be there soon.*

***

   Charly settled the girls at a table in their room overlooking the Chicago River. Happy to be out of the car, they easily settled in to puzzles and snacks of strawberries and dry Cheerios. "I'm going to wash my face and be right out, okay?"
   In stereo, they answered, "Okay, Mommy."
   With a resigned sigh, she splashed water over her face. Blindly she hunted for a towel and pressed it to her skin. Pulling it from her face, she frowned at the reflection in the mirror. Her face revealed every emotion she felt: sadness, uncertainty, pain, and fear for her future.
   "Daddy!"
   Hearing elated shrieks from the other room, she swallowed hard and dried her tears. Sucking in her emotions, she prepared to face her husband.
   She lingered in the bathroom's doorway, listening and watching from afar. *Why can't he love me the same way he loves them?*
   After what seemed like an eternity of hugs, kisses, and tickles, her husband, in his own wonderful way, resettled their girls, handing them crayons and more puzzles.
   He faced Charly.
   Do not look at me like that. His grin perpetually weakened her knees. Butterflies laughed and danced in her tummy. *But, I'm so damn mad at you! And, don't take your time wandering over here.*
   "Baby."
   She relented, allowing him to embrace her. *Dammit, and you have to smell good and feel even better! Toughen up! You're angry, remember?* She turned her face, forcing his kiss onto her cheek.

***

   After dinner in the room and getting his fill of his children, he read them one last story, tucking in the two exhausted sisters. Andy leaned over for one last good night kiss. Nothing calmed and centered him more than his girls, and not just the two little ones. Although elated to see his twins, he was even more excited and pleased to see his wife, regardless of the doghouse he'd probably reside in for some time.

His wife was under the covers in the other bedroom of the suite, on her back, her arm crossed over her eyes.

Andy gently climbed in beside her, not wanting to startle her. He hoped he'd not be rejected—at least not too severely. He slipped one arm under her neck and draped his other over her midsection, resting his head against hers. Her alluring scent rushed blood to his groin. Listening to her breathing, he wanted nothing more to roll on to her, rub himself against her, and find a way inside her.

Dammit! He didn't let her turn too far out of his hold. "Charly."

"What?"

Even though their children were fast asleep in the other room, still he kept his voice low, hoping his gentle tone would calm her irritation. "Don't shut me out."

Her voice was even and quiet. "I'm doing no such thing, Andy. I'm here, the girls are here. I wouldn't call that shutting you out."

"I thought we put this behind us."

"You did, huh?"

"Talk to me."

He could feel her holding her breath, counting to ten, preparing to temper her words.

"And just what would you like to talk about? How you've humiliated the woman you're married to? You're not home, you have no idea what people—what the media—in Milwaukee are saying about you, and most importantly about us."

"Honey—"

"Shut up." Despite the rebuke, her tone remained civil. "Isn't that what you said to me over the phone a last week when I was 'overreacting?' It's your turn to 'shut up and listen.' You show up in a high-scale magazine with nearly nude models draped all over you. It's everywhere. And I'm supposed to ignore it, slap on a smile, and not be offended, hurt, or concerned? You tell me how, Andrew Knox, you tell me how and I'll do it."

Shit...I totally fucked up this time.

"I can't go to the store without *this* in my face, magazines, whispering, the clerks in the checkout line. They all want to know if

43

our marriage is over. 'Those poor little girls.' That's the latest thing I'm hearing."

"Why do you listen to it?"

"I'm not *actively* listening to it, *It* comes to *me!* Do you realize we're a game show on some local radio station? I know *you're* in the public eye, but you didn't have to drag the rest of us in, too."

She sighed, releasing a load of pent up frustration. Quietly she mentioned, "I love you, Andy"

"I love—"

"Please," she interrupted. "I *love* you, but, I don't *like* you very much right now."

Resting his head against the back of hers, he sighed, feeling guilty and embarrassed. His voice had never been so small. "I'm sorry, Charly. I'm sorry."

"I've heard those words before. This can't be like the last time, Andy. We have too much at stake this time around, including two children. Please don't humiliate me like that. I know you love your profession, and you're lucky to have the talent to do something so many other men only fantasize about. I want you to have fun, to do and experience what is only a dream for other people. But our integrity needs to be foremost. While all the negative attention is painful, I actually don't care what *other* people think, but I have to know *you* care what *I* think."

His heart ached when she slipped from his hold.

"And, I really wanted to have sex tonight, since it's just about the right time of the month for us to get pregnant...." She left the thought floating, dissipating into the tense ether.

A bed creaked in the other bedroom.

What the fuck is wrong with me? He swiped at his eyes, wondering how he had driven his wife so far away from him.

***

The next evening, after a horrendous game, she nodded and smiled as she and Andy made their way through the lobby of the team's hotel. Fans wanting autographs were out of luck. His arms were full, weighed down by two sleeping four-year-olds. A day at the ball park, watching her husband play, together as a couple with their children, had slowly softened her anger. *If you only knew how much watching you be a dad turns me on!*

Back in the hotel room, they chuckled quietly, removing their children's layers of jackets and sweaters, and shoes. The twins never woke as their parents tended to them. Charly watched Andy give them each a lingering kiss and long look before he sighed, leaving them to their sleep.

Andy slipped into their bed, spooning up to Charly. She sighed, for the first time in a few weeks completely content, again feeling safe and loved. He "mmmed," settling in to her, and a little electrical spark warmed her low in her belly.

"Thank you for an incredible day, hon."

She turned her head over her shoulder to peer at him in the darkness. "I didn't do anything."

He kissed her gently on the mouth. "You're here, the girls are here. That always makes for a good day."

"Even if your team sucks?"

"Yeah, we do."

"You're doing your part, but I don't know about the rest of the squad. Great trade, huh?"

"Can't say it was the best move I've ever made, but you know...."

"You didn't have any control over it—either accept it or quit playing. I know. Just can't see you full-time in bib overalls in a milking parlor yet." She felt his amused smile against her cheek. "I'm sorry I overreacted. I'm sorry for how hard this has been on us."

"No, baby, you had every right to be pissed off. It won't happen again, I promise."

"Andy?"

"Yeah, hon?"

"I love you."

He cocked his head at her. "You're sure about that?" he teased.

She turned in his hold, watching as he closed his eyes and groaned when she skimmed her hands under his tank top caressing his chest. Baring his skin, she rubbed her face against his well-cut pectoral muscles. "Oh, I'm pretty sure about that." She sighed, hugging him well.

"Were you serious about what you said last night, Char? Do you want another baby? I know, eventually, Chloe will go deer hunting with me, but Bree, she'll stick her nose in the air at the thought of a camo dress."

45

She laughed aloud at his silly, but exact, description of their children. They both quieted, and she looked up at him. Even in the dark his beautiful chocolate-brown eyes twinkled in mischief. "Do *you*?" she asked.

"Course I do. There's more than enough estrogen in our house, and once they get into their teens, I'll have absolutely *no* backup! Didn't we talk about three or four?"

"That was before we had two at once."

"Well, numbers shift. We can up that to four or five, if you want."

She tried to stifle the thought, but it fell from her mouth anyway, "Well, we've *sort of* already had three." She held back the tears when he collected her in his arms. If life had gone according to plan, they'd already have been parents of three.

"I know." He encouraged her to her back. "You *are* damn cute pregnant." His warm hand clutched her tummy as he continued. "You get all pooched out and tight right here."

"That's *cute* to you?" she chided.

He moved a wayward sprig of hair from her forehead. "*You're* cute to me. You get curvy in all the right spots." He raised an eyebrow at her. "You know what that does to me!"

When he draped a long leg over hers, a growing stiffness prodded at her. *Damn, Andy, your hard dick always gets me wet!* "We better get busy then, huh?"

***

"Will you be home soon, Daddy?" Bree asked. She and her sister stood on the rail next to the dugout. The two girls were steadied by their mother behind them, as they were hugged by their father on the other side.

"Probably sooner than you think, babies." He kept his voice low, not wanting anyone around to hear him and think he was hoping his new team would be eliminated before post season play.

Glancing at the scoreboard, Charly shook her head. "I'm sure you're right on *that* account, hon." She smiled at her family. Her husband covered his daughters' faces with silly kisses, squeezing them tightly. She knew he took fatherhood seriously, making sure his children knew he loved them regardless of being physically away from them more than half the year.

"Knox!" Their surname came bellowing from dugout.

"Give me one more kiss, Chloe. You, too, Bree."

Holding her breath, she didn't want to get emotional in public, in love with the fact *he* was so in love with them.

When the hugs and kisses ended, he returned his girls to solid ground in the stands. "Wait there for Mommy, okay?" He took his wife's hand, drawing her to him.

Charly breathed him in—a scent of sweat, dust, and physical work, and a hint of some muscle balm his trainers used during the season.

Sealed in his embrace, his body still warm from the early May sun and physical work, her body tingled and her mind flooded with thoughts of their near secretive love making the night before. She bit her lip, wondering how Andy had performed so well on the field, considering their coupling had lasted until near daybreak.

His lips pressed to her ear, he sang quietly, "I know what you're thinking."

"You do?" She pressed her knees together, wanting to ward off any beginning of arousal, but the image of her husband smothering her bare body with his, her arms pinned over her head as his strength ground into her had her holding back a pant.

"Did last night do the trick? If not, with what's going on in my cup right now, I'll need to drag you into the dugout to get some relief!"

His tongue met her ear and she slumped into his hold.

"I love you."

She held in a sniffle. When he released her to look into her eyes, he smeared a tear across her cheek with a strong thumb. She tossed herself back into his hold, clinging to him tightly. "I love you, Andy, and I miss you already."

"I'll see you soon." He kissed her cheek, then her mouth. "Look at the schedule, see what looks doable, with or without the girls, okay?"

"All right."

He cocked his chin toward the stands. "This gentleman will take you to the car." With a wet smooch to her forehead he mentioned, "I gotta get going, Char."

She nodded again and let him go. "Daddy's going, girls."

"Bye, Daddy! See you on TV!"

He ruffled their hair once more and then put a hand to Charly's cheek. "Love you, babe."

Her eyes didn't leave his until he disappeared under the dugout overhang.

Chapter Five

Life returned to a new rhythm. They caught up in person any time the family could. For Charly that meant a few hours on an airplane for barely a full weekend with her husband every now and then. The twins especially loved a long weekend of baseball-related fun during July's All Star week. She loved the fact that Andy had made the prestigious squad again this season, but those Titan pinstripes still irritated the hell out of her.

The four sat together in the hotel dining room, just like any other family on a summertime vacation. Breakfast was certainly the one thing Andy truly missed with his family.

"Mommy, can Daddy see the pictures now?" Bree asked.

"It looks like you're finished with your eggs, so I suppose that will be all right. Wipe your hands first." The four year old did as her mother requested before taking her mother's phone.

"This is when we went to the zoo, Daddy."

Andy smiled, listening to his daughter's colorful description of animals large and small.

"What's this one?"

"I don't know. Mommy, what's this?" Bree held the phone up to her mother. Chloe took a look at the photo as well.

"It's a plus sign," Chloe mentioned. "We're doing adding."

"Maybe he needs to see it a little closer."

He took the phone from his daughter. A millisecond later, he understood. "Are you sure?" he choked out. When he looked at Charly, he did so through eyes blurred with tears.

She smiled at him, taking his hand. "Guess that weekend in Chicago did the trick!"

"Are you okay, Daddy?"

49

He looked at his girls, their little faces full of concern. He could only nod and kiss their foreheads. Any spoken word would cause his voice to break. After he'd calmed his girls, he turned back to his wife. "Baby." Leaving his seat, he swept her into his arms, knowing as he hugged her, he also embraced the little being growing inside her. "Thank you, honey, thank you."

"Well, *you* had something to do with it!"

Cradling her face in his hands, he asked, "How long?"

"Well." He watched as she did math in her head. "Eight, nine weeks. So let's just keep it 'in the family' for now, okay?"

"Okay." Bringing her face to his, he kissed her, long, deeply and without shame, regardless of their public situation.

"Uh, Andy. We're getting looks."

He chuckled into her neck.

"If I see a cell phone or a flash, I'm not going to be happy," she joked. Her teasing thought realized with a nearby blink of light.

"Let's see it, Chloe," Bree demanded.

"Wait, Bree, you have to push this first," Chloe answered. The two girls hovered over their mother's phone.

He put his forehead to Charly's. "Yeah, we need a few more people in the house who are more technologically advanced than we are!"

***

Summer heat, humidity, and pregnancy never made for a good combination, but in Charly's case, the three worked overtime against her. Morning sickness had settled in a week ago. But this seemed like much more than routine pregnancy complaints.

She didn't want to admit it, but she knew the exact pain which rousted her from sleep.

"No, no, no, not again." She pressed hard on her lower tummy. *Please, let it stop.* But relief didn't come.

"Mommy?" Sitting up in bed with their mother, the girls peered at her with concern.

A small hand touched her forehead, stroking hair from her face. Chloe leaned forward, her brows narrowed, obviously worried. "You're so hot, Momma." They were wise beyond their almost-five years. "Are you okay?"

Through the pain, she watched Bree, a seemingly too large

phone in her small hands.

"Gramma? Can you come over?"

Between the pain and her abdominal muscles preparing to bring up the contents of her empty stomach, passing out would have been a blessing. Her hand dropped near her children. "Give me the phone, Bree."

"Here's Gramma."

"Mom, can you come get me? It's happening again."

***

Andy slid down into the tub, steamy water bubbling near his ears. Closing his eyes, he replayed tonight's game in his head—despite having the season of his life, his performance all for naught. Most of the team sucked. *Huntington and I are doing all the work! I never thought being a Titan would be so embarrassing!*

A ping on the deck of the tub distracted him from his wallowing. He shook water from his hands and grabbed his phone. With a snicker, he shook his head as a Holstein cow's face filled the screen, an inside joke with his brother, Aaron. He tapped the screen and the text appeared.

WTF, bro?

He tapped on the accompanying file. He turned the phone horizontal so the video properly filled the screen.

Red and blue lights crisscrossed a white-lit stage. County nymph Treena Cache's high bold voice came from the speaker on his phone. The shaky cell-phone video shot zoomed in on Andy, clearly visible behind the indecently clad country singer. Microphone in one hand, his other about the bare midsection of the singer, he matched her note for note and explicit move for move.

Caught the show in KC. She waved me up on stage.

And you had to go?

She wanted me to sing with her.

Obviously, she wanted to do something else with you….

Andy narrowed his eyes at his phone. With a bit of irritation he tapped, *What's your point?*

Charly.

What about her?

How do you think she's going to feel when she sees this?

She doesn't spend much time on Facebook, YouTube, or online at all-unless it has to do with art.

You didn't answer the question. It's not a matter of if she sees it, it's a matter of when.

He rolled his eyes and shook his head, Why was everyone in his personal business? He tapped back, *Again, what is your point, Aaron?*

If you don't know what this sort of outward bullshit is doing to your marriage, then I can't say much more. Sounds like you want me to stay out of it...so I will.

A call interrupted the text volley. "Hey, Mom."

"Can you get home, Andy?"

Those words never brought good news. "What's going on?"

"Charly had a miscarriage. She's at Froedert Hospital. Call or text when you get to town."

"What?"

"Just get here. She and the girls need you."

***

Settled in the corner of the hospital room, the girls were entertained by their ten-year old cousin, Jeremy, coloring books, and Legos.

Charly rested in bed, still light-headed from pain-numbing drugs. Her mother-in-law sat nearby, offering ice chips and motherly support.

Linda Knox glanced at her phone on the bedside table. The buzz meant one thing—her youngest son had arrived. She texted back the room number and then looked at her grandchildren. "Jeremy, why don't you and the girls go for a little walk." She dug in her purse, extracting a ten dollar bill. "Do you think you can find the cafeteria? I think the girls would like some ice cream."

As expected, the young man didn't balk. He graciously accepted the bill, stuffed it in his front pocket, and put out his hands for his cousins. "C'mon Bree, c'mon Chlo." The girls willingly went with him.

Andy cracked the door of the hospital room, concerned about what he'd see and his reception from his family. "Mom?"

He'd seen that same look on his mother's face a few times in his life—like when he ripped the transmission out of a brand new F-150 pickup truck screwing around, running the vehicle through the woods near their farm, Or in high school, when he brought home an F, in, of all things, physical education. The teenager had refused to participate in gym class, saying he didn't want to wear himself out before baseball practice.

The knot in his gut pulled tighter as his mother slipped by him, saying nothing.

He had a difficult time keeping his composure. Tears bubbled in the corners of his eyes as he choked out, "Charly?"

When took her hand, she blinked at him then turned her face away.

He clutched her hand, more so to anchor himself and keep his tears riveted in place, than to possibly comfort his wife. Stroking her soft hair from her still-flushed forehead, he leaned over and kissed her temple. "I'm sorry, baby."

"For what?" She asked, her tone flat.

"That I wasn't here."

She turned her face back to where he stood, looking at her, his hand still holding hers. "It seems you were busy at the time."

He sucked in a breath, shocked, she'd never before used his profession against him. Forcing down any notion of irritation, he did the one thing he knew would erase that hurt. He moved toward his wife for an embrace, but Charly stiffened in his hold, rejecting him. Regardless, he hugged her well, even if only for his own comfort.

The girls and his nephew returned. He altered his demeanor for the sake of the kids in the room. Cups of ice cream forgotten, Breanna and Chloe piled the small containers into their cousin's grasp and ran headlong into their father's waiting hug.

They tripped over their worried questions. "Is Mommy okay? Can we go home? Are you staying, Daddy?" And the one statement which tore at his heart to the point of tears. "I'm scared, Daddy."

Clutched in his embrace, the aroma of his little girls filled his nose and evoked a strong desire to be home. In the back of his mind, a slow understanding of what transpired began to take shape, what he may have been losing, where had he gone wrong.

"It's going to be okay. Mommy's going to be all right." Kissing them both, he redirected their attention to their ice cream.

Moving back to Charly's bed, whether she wanted it or not, he kissed her again.

"The girls will keep you company. I'll be right back, hon."

Hoping for any response, his emotions dashed again when she looked away without even acknowledging he'd spoken.

He found his mother in the hallway, leaning against the wall, head down in thought or maybe prayer. His inquiry requested answers to more than just the obvious physical situation with his wife. "What the hell is going on, Mom? What did the doctors say?"

"Sit."

Her stern, inarguable tone sent his mind back to his boyhood on his family's dairy farm. A good lashing was most likely forthcoming.

"What do you think they said?" she asked rhetorically.

He shrugged, unsure where this line of discussion was headed.

"You lost a son or daughter, the girls lost a sibling, and your father and I lost another grandchild, that's what the doctors said."

He struggled to hold back tears. "It's happened before, I know."

"Andrew, that doesn't make it any easier on Charly, especially as of late."

Her tone immediately put him on the defensive. "I know I'm not home half the summer, and this year it's been pretty much all summer, but it's what I do, Mother. She knows that. It's our life. She and I have had this conversation numerous times over the past ten years plus."

She moved directly in front of his chair. "Oh, Andy." A disgusted chuckle left her mouth. "Where is your head? You're killing your wife and your marriage with your actions."

Why am I the bad guy in all this? He opened his mouth in reply, but the disciplinarian he hadn't heard in more than twenty years took control of his mother's being.

"What are you thinking, Andrew! What are you doing when you're away from home?"

Playing dumb, he ignored what he knew—the explicit photo shoot with the models earlier in the season, the suggestive dance video with Treena Cache which had gone viral. *I really don't want to have this conversation again!*

"You know damn well what you've done, Andrew." Her tone took a hard turn. "We all know what you've been doing—first that distasteful magazine spread and now a disgusting video with that singer."

Andy held back a small snort. *You people need to lighten up.* "Geez, Mom, you know how many times I've had to defend myself on this? I was all in good fun. I am not cheating on Charly, if that's what this conversation is really about." He looked back up at his mother, seeking an iota of understanding.

None came. She would refuse to understand and accept his New York Titan behavior. Without warning, her strong, callused farm-woman's hand smacked him squarely across the face.

He almost mumbled "what the fuck," but he knew that would have prompted the opposite cheek being cracked. Before he could tend to his stinging cheek, she grabbed his face in her warm palms. The comforting touch following such an angry slap focused his attention.

"You weren't raised like this. Your father and I raised you and your brothers to respect people of all kinds, especially women, and, most importantly, the women you're related to. You have inflicted some serious, and possibly irreparable, emotional harm to your wife. I'd venture to say, Andrew, even more painful than the fallout you two had before you were married. You know your father and I don't get involved in our children's business, but, this time, I can't sit back and stay out of it. This not only hurt her. Watching her being hurt by someone we love—*you*—hurts all of us as a family. And when that happens, it's my responsibility as a parent to say something."

"Mom-"

"Be quiet, you *will* hear what I have to say. Get your shit together, Andrew Knox. Step up and truly be a husband and a father. I'm not saying you don't *provide*. You do. You've done very well in that regard. And, I'm not saying you don't love Charly and the girls. What I am saying, is right now, your actions are disrespectful to them, to your brothers, and to your father and me. And you better be glad, I'm the one who had this conversation with you. Your father would have given you more than a smack and told you things I know you never want to hear—quit playing around, quit playing with your life, your family's emotions, quit playing all these games, *including baseball*, and come home and be the husband and dad we *know* you are!"

Before he could respond, even agree with his mother on so many points, she gently kissed his head and walked away.

***

Charly took the few steps from the garage into the house slowly, still a bit sore, still a bit wobbly. She smiled at her girls. They refused to leave her side, clutching the hem of her shirt. In their little minds, they were helping, steadying her, playing nursemaid.

Andy settled a warm hand on her hip. His touch comforted but at the same time irritated her. *Don't dote. I'll have to deal with this by myself when you leave.* Heading toward their bedroom, she took a turn into her office.

"No, you don't." Andy steered her back in her original direction.

"I have things to do."

"Whatever it is, can wait. C'mon, now."

She wanted to plop into bed, but she knew that would be a bad, probably painful move. She lowered herself to the mattress. Andy stepped up and lifted her legs up on the comforter. *How can I stay mad when he's being so sweet?*

The twins scrambled up on the bed, wanting to be close to their mother.

"No jumping, please," Andy insisted.

"Ladies," she addressed her girls, "would you go in the kitchen, get me a cup of ice and some soda? Just bring me the can, okay?" Her twins nodded, shimmied off the bed, and took off for the kitchen.

She didn't want the attention but allowed him to take off her shoes, fluff pillows, and tuck a blanket in around her. Heading to put away her footwear, he stopped abruptly in front of the wall-mounted flat screen television.

He traced the crack in the panel, clearly an impact starburst, and followed the webbing of the glass with his fingers. "What happened to the TV?"

I don't need this discussion right now, considering I still feel like hammered crap, but since you asked. "I broke it."

"How?"

"When I flung the alarm clock at it."

"I know you don't like getting up for work some days, but that's a bit extreme." Slight entertainment colored his statement.

"No, I threw the clock at it two nights ago watching video of you nearly fucking Treena Cache. It was all over Sports Center. I'm surprised *you* didn't see it." *Now get the fuck out of my sight before I throw something at you.*

"Charly...."

"Don't say anything." She glared a hole right through him,

watching guilty red creep up from the collar of his T-shirt and work its way up his neck, "I don't want to have a conversation right now. I want to put my head down, rest a little, and cry because I lost another baby."

"Char...."

Any beginning of explanation or apology stopped when Bree and Chloe returned to the room. One carried a plastic tumbler filled with ice, the other a can of soda in one hand and a box of crackers in the other.

"Here, Mommy."

"And, you brought me crackers, too. Thank you, that's so thoughtful, babies." They crawled up on the bed again, tending to their mother.

"Mommy's going to take a nap. You want to go to the store with me?" Andy asked.

"We'll stay here with Mommy. She needs us," Bree answered.

Charly watched as shock and sadness painted his face, his heart breaking with that answer.

Andy left the room to finally put away her shoes and mentally flog himself in a private setting. Returning to the bedroom, he looked at his bed, on it *everything* in the world he loved. But, it seemed, *nothing* that loved him right now.

He drove to the nearest grocery, went in, and walked out with staples: milk, bread, string cheese the girls liked, and Charly's favorite wine. *She won't crack it for a few days, until she's free of meds, but, yeah, she deserves to.* Thankfully, he got in and out without being noticed. His phone *pinged* in the cup holder. "Please, let it be someone friendly," he mumbled, Sighing, he was relieved when he saw Casey Rupp's mug on the screen. "Casey!"

"Stopped by the hotel in K.C. Blake told me you were called home. Everything all right?"

Andy bit down hard on his bottom lip, holding in the emotion. No one but his wife knew how her miscarriages affected him. "Charly had another miscarriage."

"Oh, man, I'm so sorry. How's she doing?"

"She's home. The girls are playing nurse."

"Where are you?"

"Sitting in a Piggly Wiggly parking lot. Just ran to the store."

"What's going on, Knox, seriously."

I can't hide shit from you, can I? "Oh"—hearing the admission come from his own mouth made the situation even more dire—"I fucked up again."

"That little video that's all over the place?"

"I—"

"Andy, Andy, Andy...."

"I know."

"You gotta—"

"Don't *tell* me I have to make this right. Don't you think I already know that?"

"We've had this conversation, Knox. Shit like this isn't worth ruining a marriage over."

"What am I missing here, Casey? Why do I put myself in these situations?"

"Seven year itch, boredom, the excitement of being"—Casey put on his best stadium announcer hat— "*Andy Knox, shortstop, New York Titans.* You seem to be buying into that New York shit, when you know you're just a farmer's kid from Sheboygan County. Only *that* farmer's kid has a drop-dead gorgeous, smart as a whip wife who's terribly in love with him and two little girls who adore the shit out of him. For some reason, he's not returning the favor."

He watched clouds brood over Lake Michigan, an August storm on the horizon.

"Andy?"

"I'm here."

"Did you contact her?"

"Who?"

"Madame Eve and the 1Night Stand agency. I told you about it months ago. I'm telling you, she *can* help."

***

"Bath time went well, and no fussing when I put them to bed." Andy sat on the edge of the bed next to his wife. "Hopefully, they'll sleep through the thunder." He offered her a mug of tea, but she relieved him of his bottle of Spotted Cow beer instead. Beer and lorazepam? "Maybe you should—" The look she shot him shut him up immediately.

She took a few sips and then placed the bottle on the nightstand. "Is there anything else I should know, Andy?" Her voice came out slow, steady, devoid of emotion.

"About what?"

"About anything—about you, your life away from home, about why there may be a reason I shouldn't trust you anymore?"

"Charly, I'm not sure what you mean."

"I mean, if you're going to do 'the dance' you used to do *only* with me with someone else, and let the whole world see it, well I need to ask if there anything I should know. Anyone else on your 'list,' I need to know about? Will you be hooking up with Miranda Lambert sometime soon?"

"C'mon now."

"What about *my* list? Wanna know who's on *my* list?"

He contemplated stopping her when she reached for the beer, but thought better of it. He didn't answer, just watched—the long pull on the ale, her gray eyes, stormy as the weather outside.

"I didn't think so."

Will playing this game make you feel better, Charly? "I do, tell me." He moved closer to her on the bed, his legs resting against hers. "Who are your five?" He focused on her eyes. They weren't tracking too precisely. *Beer and meds....*

"Well, number five, this cute guy I knew in high school. You might know him. Andy Knox?"

"C'mon, babe, don't...."

"Number four," she continued, "this guy I knew in college. We didn't go to the same school, but we saw each other as much as we could. I think you were best buds with him. Andy Knox."

He sighed, looking at his hands.

"Three, an amazingly hot shortstop for the Breakers. Great number, too—twenty-seven. *KNOX* on his back—broad shoulders, narrow hips, great ass. I think you know him—Andy Knox. Two, the handsome man I married, Andrew Knox." Her voice cracked. "Number one, the father of my children." Leaning toward him, she took his hand, squeezing to the point of discomfort. Tears cascaded along her cheeks. "Do you see why this is so hard for me? While your list has always been unattainable, you nearly *fucked one* of them live and in color! You're now in a position to be in *their* presence, when the one person who *is* on my list, *isn't*–" Releasing his hand, she uncovered herself, gingerly lifted herself from the bed, and disappeared into the bathroom.

The door clicked shut behind her, and his heart broke as he

listened to her sobs.

She watched as Andy kissed, hugged, and tickled his girls good-bye. Ready to stand her ground, she still took his hand and followed him out of the house. She stood next to his car, looking at her feet, not wanting to look into his brown eyes.

"Charly?" He touched her chin, and she tried desperately to hold tears in place. "I'm sorry, baby. I'm sorry about everything."

She shook her head, not wanting to hear his apology. "Don't. I don't want to talk about it anymore. We can't settle this in forty-eight hours, Andy. Go do what you do. We'll figure it out at the end of the season."

In one instant, she loved and hated being in his embrace. Warm and strong, his arms felt wonderful about her, the excitement of how he could control her with his strength. At the same time, bile bubbled in her gut. *If I had the strength, I'd give you a good shove right now, Andrew Knox.* Relenting, she relaxed into him.

Obviously relieved, he hugged her more diligently, his breath against her ear. "I love you, Charly. I'll never hurt you again, I promise. I *will* make this right." His forehead to hers, he asked, "You gonna be all right?"

Nodding, she mumbled through her tears. "Yes."

"I'll call you when I get to...um...."

"Baltimore."

He shook his head and smiled, "What would I do without you?" He nudged her chin with his, brushing his lips against hers.

She lifted her face and allowed him to kiss her. The buss was long, warm, and deeper than they'd shared in some time, until she broke it off. "Go on."

"I love you."

She didn't balk as he kissed her again. "You, too."

He squeezed her a last time, his lips against her ear, "I promise you, Charly, I'm going to do everything in my power to be the husband you deserve." A smooch to her forehead and he was gone.

Chapter Six

At the end of a long summer and one hundred sixty games, in two days he'd be home. Certainly ready for the season to end, Andy closed and zipped the last of his larger travel bags, snapping a lock onto the zipper. Handing the three pieces of luggage over to a courier, he tipped the man well.

Before he could close the door to his summer, home-away-from-home apartment, he heard someone call his name. "Mr. Knox!"

Impeccably dressed, immensely well-groomed, the young man stopped at the door and held out an official-looking envelope. "Andrew Knox. Delivery for you, sir."

I'm not expecting anything. He took the packet. It was unlike any he'd seen before—cream colored heavy parchment, sheathed in a clear sleeve. "Wait," digging into his jeans, he extracted a ten dollar bill.

"Thank you, sir, but I cannot accept a tip." With a sincere nod, he continued, "Enjoy your day."

He watched him walk away. Once he was well down the corridor, curiosity goading him, he began to gently open the seal on the plastic sleeve. *Wait, if this is what I think it is, it's about fucking time!* Only to be interrupted.

"Hey, Knoxville," his teammate, pitcher Blake Huntington, called from a few doors down.

"Hunts, what's up?"

"You up for some breakfast?" Blake asked. "You know, a mimosa or two to celebrate the 'how-the-hell-did-I-end-up-with-the-Titans-during-their-worst-season-ever-get-me-outta-here-and-back-to-flyover-country!'"

Damn, he sure summed that up well! Well, he understands,

he's a Michigander. "Not that you didn't try, Blake, you pitched a helluva season."

"And, you sir, saved me a lot of runs. And a stellar batting season, but even with you hitting the way you did, no one else was!"

"Too true."

"So, breakfast?"

"Would love to but I got a pile of shit to do before I bug out."

The pitcher thumped him on the shoulder wholeheartedly. "I hear ya."

"Catch up with you later, Blake."

Back in his apartment, Andy looked around at leftover shit that wasn't his. *Why do all furnished apartments look the same, even the upscale ones?* A lovely, familiar aroma caught his attention. Carefully, he slipped a finger under the opening, removing the expensive stationary from its protection. *Mmm, smells like Charly!*

Opening the flap, he retrieved its contents—two more envelopes and a letter.

Mr. Knox,

Thank you for contacting my office. It is with utmost pleasure I am able to tell you, I can most certainly assist you with your predicament.

My utmost condolences on the end of a long and arduous eight months, both professionally and personally.

But, you do, however, have a few tasks before you return home.

First: Visit Tiffany & Company on Fifth Avenue. Johanna is expecting you. If you have a photo of your wife, please bring it. Johanna is exceptionally talented in selecting the perfect gift. With what you've shared with me, I would suggest diamonds (and lots of them).

Second: Study the enclosed material as it pertains to communication and sharing.

Third: Share your fears, downfalls. Your wife loves you; she wants you to be honest.

Fourth: Flowers.

Fifth: Touch. It doesn't have to be sex, but just a physical reminder you're with her.

Sixth....

Scanning this thorough to-do list, he began to understand his unintended neglect. Life happened, children happened, and in love changed. But, if he wanted to keep the fire stoked, make their life better, secure and trustworthy in every aspect, he'd have to re-incorporate the little nuances that, years ago, had led them to love.

He understood why this agency was so expensive, and how much more it would cost him to secure the remainder of his life with the woman he loved.

***

Thank God, I'm home. He'd never been so glad to *leave* a city!

Although, now thankfully behind him, the final two games of the season were as bad as any of the embarrassing losses the Titans had suffered, but the team *had* set a two records: worst attendance in the franchise's history and worst record for the team. If there was *any* upside, Andy had played *extremely* well, despite the time away from Charly and the girls, and their irritation with one another as a couple.

He relished the slowing drone of the private jet's engines. *Next time I'm on a plane, it's for a family* vacation!

Per the suggestions from Casey's professional contact, he planned on surprising his wife. He'd told Charly he wouldn't return to Wisconsin immediately after game 162, instead he left her to believe he'd be on the first flight home in the morning.

He came in through the garage like he had thousands of times in the past. The house smelled like home, a combination of fresh coffee, a fragrance of little girl hair, and the woman he loved. From somewhere deep in the house he heard Italian, his wife up late selling art to someone across the globe. *God. I love it when she fucks in Italian!*

Cracking the door to Chloe and Bree's room, their beds were empty. *In our bed, again, I'm sure.* Down the hall, the door to the master bedroom was slightly ajar. There they were, his two little girls—one sprawled in every direction taking up most of the California-king-sized bed, the other angelically sleeping on her side, hands clasped near her beautiful face as if she'd just finished saying her prayers. Shaking his head, he smiled at them. With a sigh, he swore they were babies eight months ago, now they seemed to be near teenagers, even though they were still the same four-year-olds he hadn't seen much of since February.

He made his way to Charly's office.

"Salve, buon giorno!"

Peeking around the doorframe, he watched her as she tapped furiously on her laptop. *If you only knew how you take my breath away, baby!* Feet tucked under her butt, hair piled upon her head in a messy bun, she'd gotten up in the middle of the night to work. *Damn, if she only knew how she fills out ratty sweats and a washed-out Green Bay Packers denim button-down turns me on! Wait, per the saving-my-marriage instructions, I'll need to* tell *her that from now on. Rupp's contact is sure full of great advice!*

She scared the daylights out of him when she shrieked, surprised by his presence and a dozen roses in the doorway. "Andy!"

Getting up from the desk, she looked more delicious than he'd remembered. Her arms about his middle, she squeezed him. How he'd missed those gray eyes staring into his. Any irritation from the past months seemed to have dissipated.

"I thought you were coming home tomorrow."

"Couldn't wait," he replied, kissing her forehead.

A flickering TV distracted him. "You're watching the game?"

"Only missed two or three all season, honey. Couldn't watch it live. The girls and I needed a nap so I caught the replay—had to get up anyway to call Rome. That was the *ugliest* game of the season, I swear." Her soft had caressed his cheek, "And, I also see you haven't shaved in the past few days."

Smiling, he kissed her forehead. "A couple hundred dollar fine is worth the price to bring home a properly attired face."

"Well, thank you!" Releasing him, she took the blood-red roses from his grasp, "Roses? There haven't been red roses in this house since the girls were born."

Yeah, well, that's gonna change, honey!

She cocked her head toward the kitchen. "C'mon, I'll make you something to eat."

"You watched the games?" he questioned again, following her down the hall.

Settling the flowers into a vase, she put them in the middle of the kitchen table, pulling out a chair for him. "Had to catch you when I could. Just because I'm not crazy about the team doesn't mean I'm not *crazy* about you."

He shook his head, he *had* been missing so many signals this season, and maybe he *hadn't* assured her of what he knew and felt, that he was ultimately and completely in love with her.

"Leftover lasagna okay?" she placed a chilled Spotted Cow, his favorite, in front of him.

"Do you want a glass, hon?"

Before she could turn back to the cupboards, he took her hand, bringing her into his lap. *Damn you smell wonderful...wait, say it.* "I love you." Snugging her into his hold, he whispered, "You smell so good."

"Love you, too." She kissed his forehead, a feeling he'd missed, "But you're gonna hate me tomorrow."

He looked into her face, knowing there was *nothing* under the sun she could do to solicit such an emotion.

"I forgot to tell you about the law enforcement benevolent dinner."

"Tomorrow night?"

She nodded.

"Not a problem," he assured her, "if it means you're gonna get all swanked up!"

"Well, so are you. Black tie or equivalent." Requesting he release her, she moved through the kitchen, getting his late dinner.

"I love you, Charly. You know that, don't you?"

"I'm *pretty sure* I know." She winked.

A steaming plate of pasta in front of him, he dug in. Homemade, smothered in freshly shaved Parmigiano-Reggiano. He smiled. He was home. The only thing he needed was....

"Garlic bread? You want olive oil?"

He nodded, unable to answer, hungrier than he thought. This beat any plate from the best Italian joints in NYC, mostly because the server's little ass, clad in washed-out yoga pants, distracted him so.

"Hungry much?" She placed another piece of bread on his plate so he could mop up the remainder of the marinara.

He watched her while she watched him eat. How he'd missed her little contented smile. She turned him on just sitting there, being attentive. She sipped out of the same bottle he drank from, and he fell in love with her all over again.

She tipped the bottle toward him, and he took it and drained the last of the ale. "C'mere."

As he welcomed her into his lap, she settled astride him, her arms wrapped about his shoulders.

"I missed you, Andy. I missed you all season."

Cuddling his wife, he whispered to her, "Do you know how much I missed *you*?" She didn't flinch as he slipped his hand into her sweats, caressing her.

"Andy."

Damn, the way you sigh, turns me on...no, wait, aloud, Knox, out loud. "I love it when you breathe my name like that, Charly." He kissed her behind the ear and felt her shiver in his embrace. Shoving the dishes out of the way, he lifted his wife and plopped her ass on the kitchen table.

"Andy!" He leaned into her, laying her on the table. His strong fingers slipped under the waistband of her sweats, easing them from her hips and legs. "What about the—"

"Sound asleep halfway across the house."

He grabbed her hips, sliding her closer to the edge of the table. He opened her legs, grazing her skin with his hands. She whimpered at the small prickles of his whiskers on the skin of her inner thighs.

He feathered his lips across her skin and palmed her lower tummy, holding her steady.

"Do you have any idea how much I *love* your pussy?"

Any answer, sarcastic, silly, seductive, or otherwise, was rendered silent. She could only moan and move as his hot tongue bathed her from vagina to clit.

"Andy," she panted when his oral attention ceased. Breathing heavily, she found him poised above her, unbuttoning her denim shirt. She sucked in a breath when the air hit her nipples, only to give way to a groan as he took each breast into his strong hands then leaned in to give them long licks.

He crept up closer to her, resting his face in her neck. "Baby, you had a rack before we were married, but, *damn,* since the girls were born!" Only the jingling of belt buckle opening broke the silence. "It's okay, isn't it? You're healed and...."

"Yes."

"Then, c'mere, darlin'."

She didn't have to move much, his strength lifting her from the table and holding her above his lap until she grasped his thick cock, aiming him. A bay of a moan left her when he impaled her on it.

"You are so fucking wet."

He smiled at her. She fell into eyes of brown so deep, honest, and faithful that, despite the erotic situation they were in, she teared up. His deep, rumbling groan purred against her neck, strong hands secured her hips, forcing her down, holding her to him as he moved deep within her. Despite his powerful clench, she still tried desperately to move.

She clung to him, her cries seemed to spur his arousal.

Changing the dynamic, he flexed his powerful thighs and glutes lifting them from the chair. His huge, stiff dick moved where he directed. He ground his hips, side to side, fore and back, and in a circle. She moaned uncontrollably with his movement.

He snickered in her ear. "Uh, I guess you've missed the *happy dance,* huh?"

His hips and cock continued with their arousing movement, the same way he swayed and moved to the music performing with his bar band, only *this* dance was for *her.* He moved on her more urgently, the table legs scraping against the tile floor. When she reached for him, he complied, cradling her head in his hands.

At this moment, she could get no nearer to him—physically, emotionally, or spiritually. Her mind spinning with physical and mental sensation, she had no control over herself, she arched against the tabletop, crying out an enormous piercing wail, a sound reserved only for him.

She shook in his embrace, the strength of her orgasm depleting her of energy. She clung to him.

"Aw, shit, baby!" Then he was still.

She relished in his nearly two hundred pounds of dead weight atop her, his breathing deep and heavy as if he'd just stretched a double to third base.

"I love you," he whispered.

Why the situation struck her funny, she didn't know, but she couldn't contain the sudden onslaught of giggles.

Still panting, he asked, "What?"

"Your mom, Andy, your mother."

He pulled from her neck abruptly, staring into her face, confused. "My mom, Charly...you're thinking of my mom *right now*?"

Tilting her head back, her bare breasts jiggling with laughter, she tried to contain herself. She cleared her eyes of entertained tears. "I can just hear her, honey. 'Do you *eat* from that table?'"

His face once again in her neck, his warm tongue bathed her

skin. "Mmm, I think the answer to that question would be a resounding yes!"

"Daddy, you're so...*pretty*!" Standing on the plump sofa cushions, steadying herself on the backrest, Breanna expressed awe at her father's appearance.

Andy checked himself in a mirror, straightening his white silk tie that didn't need any correction. *Damn, I do look good!* He finger-combed his close-cropped hair and smoothed his returning beard and mustache.

"I can see why Mrs. Knox *swoons* every time you get super dressed up," the sitter teased.

"Daddy, Daddy!" Chloe had joined her sister on the cushions, Kristen with a protective arm about their jammie-clad bottoms making sure they didn't tumble backwards off the couch.

As he ruffled their curls, the little ones touched their father's silver vest, eyes big. "Shiny," one said quietly.

Please tell me her hands are clean! Last thing I need is anything sticky on this suit!

Smoothing the dark-gray fabric of his jacket, he patted the pocket, making sure he'd remembered to slip Johanna-from-Tiffany's-selected gift into it.

The sound of heels clicking on oak floors drew his attention to the hall.

Breanna and Chloe looked past their father for a better view of their mother. "Mommy!" they squealed in unison.

He wolf-whistled at his wife. "Wow, honey!" He put one hand over his heart, his breath vacuumed from his chest at seeing the woman he loved more than anything in the world, including baseball.

Her version of the little black dress was stunning—a full, frilly skirt, mid-thigh, strapless, with a belted waist. It fit exquisitely. He was certain her "stylist," Paul, wouldn't have her buying off the rack. The flowing fabric caressed her curves lovingly, showing off her lean yet womanly figure. Its length enhanced her beautiful legs.

Gorgeous, honey, but how soon can I get you out *of it!* Beaming, he breathed, "Look at you, baby. Just *look* at you!"

She shook her head, soft light-brown tendrils framed her face. She barely needed makeup—she was *that pretty*.

Coming to her, taking her hands, kissing her cheek, careful not to smudge her foundation, he whispered in her ear, "Are you wearing anything I can get my hands into under the table?"

Challenge colored her tone. "You'll have to find out."

Taking her hand, he settled her into a chair. Slipping the signature robin's egg blue box from his pocket, he placed it in her hands. She looked at him with a shrug. "Open it."

Her hand flew to her mouth, shocked at the box's contents.

Perfect reaction.

Nestled in dark fabric was a lovers' knot pendant of diamonds. Removing it from the box, he caressed her bare shoulders as he secured the gift about her neck.

She rose from the chair, moving to a nearby mirror. Moving behind her, he watched as she touched the gems.

"This is too much, Andrew. It's beautiful."

He didn't care if his children observed and was oblivious to a possibly peeking babysitter. His lips met the curve of her neck. "Not nearly as beautiful as you," he whispered, "Nothing's too much or too good for you." He touched the hollow of her throat with his finger, tracing her skin down to where the pendant hung. Touching it, he gazed into the mirror and into his wife's eyes. *Get it right, Knox. She won't think it sounds sappy.* "Look, it has no beginning and no end. It's how I love you, Charlotte. I don't know when I started and I know I always will."

Their intense quiet moment dissipated with Breanna's shriek. "Pictures, pictures!" The girl found the teen's phone and handed it to Chloe, who hopped up and down in playful insistence.

"Put it down, Chlo." Charly looked at her daughter in the way only an irritated mother can.

"Okay, Mommy."

"You ask before you touch Kristen's things."

He held back a snicker when his younger daughter turned to her sitter and asked, "Kisten, take a picture?"

"Please?" The sixteen-year-old tickle-poked the girl.

"Peese?"

"Okay."

Putting a firm, caressing hold around his wife's waist, directing her in front of the mantle. He kissed her cheek, breathing in the aroma of the woman he adored more than *anything* else in the world. As Kristen clicked away with her phone, he whispered, "Is this dinner over yet?" He clutched her a bit more tightly, pressing himself to her.

Smiling broadly, Andy held back a snicker, wondering how quickly the two of them could get through appetizers, dinner, and small talk and get back home and get into bed... hopefully after the girls were tucked in and fast asleep.

***

It had been a lovely evening, a beautiful venue, excellent cause, and the company outstanding. Leaning over and speaking quietly to Andy, Charly excused herself.

Before she could stand, *he* did with a hand out to help her from her seat.

He kissed her cheek and whispered, "Come back quick, I miss you already."

She hurried to the ladies' room, thankful every stall was empty. She took the farthest one from the entry. In her head, somehow it provided more privacy.

What is going on? She couldn't think. Sitting in a bathroom stall, she hadn't gone there to "do business," but rather to sort out her feelings. She dabbed at her eyes with a wadded tissue.

He's so attentive. What is wrong with him? Although he'd always been a wonderful husband, this event had her second-guessing the man to whom she was married. He was always a gentleman, but since he'd last been in her presence for any extended period of time, he'd changed.

Sure, he'd been affectionate with her in public, but, tonight, a different approach—*always* a touch, the hold of a hand, a lingering caress of her thigh during dinner, his warm hand on her back as they mingled.

I'm included in everything. If a partygoer wanted to talk baseball, it wasn't without her. *He dragged me into every picture. How did I end up at the* top *of the food chain?* The beautiful gift of jewelry, his affection in front of the girls *and* the babysitter, so many kind words and compliments, and the caring insistence of his lovemaking last night... *I don't understand this.*

He looks at me, when I'm talking, like he's actually interested in what I have to say, even something he knows nothing about.

And, he's read more than just Art for Dummies. He had at least one intelligent thing to say about every piece—without hesitation.

Usually, he's glazed over halfway through the first one!
What the hell is going on?
Her face in her hands, she stifled a choked realization into the wadded tissue. Her stomach churned, the exquisitely prepared dinner she'd consumed some ninety minutes ago threatening to return. Morbid memories flooded to the front of her mind.

No, this can't be the same situation as Mom's. It'd been an odd gesture, her father showering her mother with attention *and* a just-the-two-of-them vacation. The twelve-year-old caught somewhere in between thrilled her father was with them and terrified at what the end of their week alone together would bring. It was the best and worst seven days of her short life. But, left with her mother's good friend, she'd calmed and opened up to her '*Aunt Rita.' She took such good care of me. It was quiet, no arguing, fighting, breaking things. I had such a good week there—the week Dad doted on Mom and took her on a trip. His last hurrah before leaving us for good.* "No!" The echo of her own voice reverberating off the fancy tile of the ladies room startled her. *This* can't *be what Andy's doing—he* promised.

She sat for a while, not knowing what to think. Good and bad paraded through her consciousness. Each thought had opposite sides; each side held equal weight. *He's doting because he loves me—he's doting because he's leaving me. He was so anxious to make love last night, because he loves me—he wanted to "do me" one more time before he bolts! He loves the girls, but he wasn't around this summer to take care of them.*

I can't stay in here all night! Putting a stranglehold on her emotions, she left the stall, checking herself in the mirror. Again, she dabbed her eyes, smoothed foundation, and checked for any running mascara. *Just enjoy it!*

***

The limo picked them up outside the venue. He kissed her cheek as she slid inside. After a short chat with the driver, he dove in beside her, the heavy door of the Lincoln closing soundly, sealing them in.

She seems nervous. She nibbled on her bottom lip and tossed him a wink. Leaning over in her seat, she toyed with the switch controlling the dark window between the driver's and passengers' compartments. With a *whir*, it went down completely. Leaning through the opening, she spoke quietly to the driver. The window went back up.

What is *she up to?* Not concerned, but curious in an entertained way, he leaned back into the leather seat. With a sigh and a grin, he couldn't be more proud, recalling how well she had handled all of tonight's attention; not only people looking at her because she was so incredibly stunning, but the attention of being beautiful *and* the wife of a Gold Glove-winning ballplayer. Party guests wanted to talk and visit with *him*, but he gently didn't allow it unless she was part of the meeting/greeting and conversation. It was ultimately important to him that those wanting to meet him knew, and that *she* knew, she was as much a part of him as baseball.

She snuggled up beside him, draped her long, toned legs over his, and slipped off her heels. He relaxed into her when she rested her head on his shoulder, kissing his ear, his breath coming faster as her hand rested high on his upper leg. "Andy, what have you been up to?"

Resting his head against hers, he wondered, "What do you mean, honey?" He sucked in a breath as her finger made circles along his inseam.

Her voice was low, whispery. "Oh, I don't know, your sudden knowledge of art, modern, classic, and otherwise. I thought for a moment you were going to give a lecture on Dale Chihuly. I'll make sure to tell Emmy Klaussen you think her work is so much better." The tip of her tongue swirled about his ear. "That made me so *hot*."

Follow the instructions. "I just admire what you do and what you know, Charly."

He thought he heard a stifled whine of shock. *Not that I'd be surprised. Hell, I don't think I ever told her I'm amazed by her intelligence and everything else she is that I am not.*

"I love you, number twenty-seven. And you'll *always* be that number to me," she whispered.

Closing his eyes, he attempted to temper his breathing as she continued to caress him through the expensive fabric of his tuxedo pants.

Her obviousness surprised him. "Charly, babe," he grunted, stunned by her overt affection, especially here, in the backseat of a limousine after a classy affair. "What're you doin' to me?"

She quieted his question with a deep kiss. Her hand found his and directed it under the chiffon of her skirt, to the closing of her one-piece bustier undergarment. The snaps clipped open. He found her wet and ready; there was no turning back.

Before he could slip fingers into that hot, wonderful place, she pulled away. Kneeling before him, her gray eyes never leaving his, she unfastened his belt, popped the button, and unzipped his pants. He moaned through her gentle digging until she fully exposed him.

She lifted herself and wrapped her arms about his neck. She rubbed herself on him. He buried his face in her cleavage, breathing in her subtle perfume and sex. She kissed him again and then held his face in her hands.

Looking into her gray eyes, he had no doubt about the utter seriousness of her venture. He brought his mouth to hers, kissing her intensely, and his other hand under her lacey undergarment. Gripping him securely, Charly moved atop him. "Fuck, baby." She thrust herself on him again and again.

Although supremely turned on, he couldn't help but watch his wife enjoy herself.. "Do you *know* how much I'm in love with you?" As if having to make that point, he grabbed a handful of her thick hair, controlling her, kissing her with indescribable passion. His pelvic, gluteus, and thigh muscles continued to move him gently in and out of her. His face in her neck, he felt her struggling to writhe on him, and he clutched his wife tightly as he burst within her.

The feral nature of this encounter had them both sprinting to the finish.

"Andy!"

Not wanting any of this to end, he gripped her waist firmly, holding her down on him as she convulsed. Before either of them had fully recovered, he tickled her ear with his tongue. "I know a place where we can have some more fun."

***

Hand in hand they entered the grand Pfister Hotel in downtown Milwaukee. When Charly tried to head toward the reception desk, Andy clasped her elbow and herded her straight into the elevator.

He held up a keycard. "Already taken care of, Charlotte."

Unsure where her *old* husband had gone, still she was going to relish every moment of this evening. And considering the way the summer had played out, she would have the fun they'd missed, *and* not concern herself, at least for the moment, as to where their somewhat irritated relationship was headed.

With a little shove, she forced his back against the wall of the car. As quickly as she'd done in the limo, his fly was opened and she grasped him.

"Hey!"

Not one for extremely high heels, she'd donned four-inches-plus tonight. The extra height came in handy as she turned her back to him, lifted the skirt of her dress slightly and wedged his growing hardness between her legs. "Comfortable?"

His strong arm wrapped about her waist, pulling her nearer. "What the fuck, Charly!"

Gently, she ground herself against him, swayed her hips, feeling him hardening more and more.

"Are you giving me an art lesson?" he breathed in her ear.

"What do you mean?"

"*Frottage*, honey. Getting a picture from taking charcoal or pastel and *rubbing* it over something." He now ground himself into her. "Although, I'm thinking we're using that technique for a different outcome right now."

She found herself tighter in his hold. *Wait, who's doing the moving here? And where are you getting all this art knowledge?*

The car came to a bouncy stop. Glancing at the floor indicator, they were nowhere near the twenty-third floor.

She smoothed her skirt, making sure they were both properly covered. They stood, unmoving, as the door opened and an older couple stepped inside. All four nodded a congenial hello. The silence was excruciating.

The floor indicator lit up nineteen, and the car stopped again. Before the doors opened, the man turned to them, giving them a slight squint.

"I'm hoping you're out of those terrible pinstripes soon, Andy Knox. We need you back here in Milwaukee." Then he put out his hand.

His left arm tightening around her middle, Andy reached out with is right to shake the admirer's hand. "Well, thank you. I can only hope."

"Best of luck. Good night, then."

She barely contained her giggling, hoping the elevator doors were closed before she burst out laughing. She calmed in short order as Andy's lips met the curve of her neck.

"Good thing you had those baby wipes in your purse, or that'd guy have our 'juice' all over his hand!"

"Baby wipes or not, do you know how difficult it is to look distinguished, walking into an upscale place like this with your jizz leaking down my leg?" The car stopped on the twenty-third floor. She reached for the "close door" button. "This is a classy place, Mr. Knox. You'd best be putting your penis away."

The sentiment hit him just the way she'd hoped. His laugh filled the small space as he tucked and zipped. Satisfied with his appearance, she removed her finger from the button, the doors opened and they headed to their room.

At the door, Andy slipped the card into the key reader and the lock popped open. She'd forgotten the exact room number at the Pfister where they'd spent their honeymoon, but when he scooped her up in his arms, taking her over the threshold, the memories of this room flooded back.

"You thought I forgot, didn't you?"

Her face nestled in his neck, she nodded. *What is up with you tonight, Andy Knox?*

"Are you kidding? I thought you screwed the skin off my dick that night."

Back on her feet, she leaned into him. "I couldn't walk for a week." In his embrace, she closed her eyes, not wanting to let go. It felt like he didn't want to either.

Opening her eyes, shock filled her. Photos were scattered about the room. *Our life, it's everywhere.*

From the earliest days of them knowing one another in high school to a photo taken less than an hour ago. Moving about the room, touching the pictures, she relived each moment in them. The warmth of a calf on the Knox farm. Andy's laugh as she tried to bottle feed the bovine. A hot August day, his sweaty hug on the field of Milwaukee's ballpark. Her husband goofing, posing as Michelangelo's David outside the *Accademia* Gallery in Florence. The new father, tears in his eyes, holding their newborn daughters.

He squeezed her shoulders. "Don't cry, baby." He kissed her cheek at the same time he unzipped her dress. "Charly, you have the most beautiful skin."

Turnabout is fair play. Turning in his hold, she folded back the lapels of his jacket. Getting the message, he took it off and, as he draped it over an upholstered chair, she began on the buttons of his vest then shirt. She carefully undid his tie and stripped it from around his neck. Time slowed; his removal of his vest, shirt, and tank top took time. Her eyes never left his as he slowly stripped. He took her hands, bringing them to the buckle of his belt and *she* nearly buckled, stunned by his meticulous removal of clothing.

"Go on," he breathed.

Her hands trembled. They'd trembled in the same manner when she undressed him the first time they'd made love. His fingers were electric on her skin as he unclipped the front closure of her torso-covering undergarment.

She stripped out of it and kicked out of her heels, at the same time he shed his tux trousers and everything else he wore.

Forced onto the bed by his tall, strong body, she gave up trying to understand everything that had transpired this evening. She stopped trying to decipher the message, ceased wondering about his intentions, quit second-guessing his love for her. Her rational self checked out, giving in to his long, deep kisses and his strong hands caressing every part of her body.

Chapter Seven

Her insistence in the limo had screwed with his mind and libido, but, watching her now, a whole new level sexual enlightenment. She seemed another woman, yet *his* Charly, only she fucked him in a whole new way.

He loved watching her as they made love. Astride him, she forced herself down on him as he pushed up. Her hands always wandered, touching herself, touching him, playing, reaching to massage him, spur him on. Tonight, however, she did something he'd never seen before.

Mesmerized, he couldn't take his gaze from her. She rolled her fingers over her nipples, pinching, pulling. Her moan amazed him. Then, her eyes locked with his, she cupped one of her ample breasts, moving it upward. She bent her head and flicked her tongue over a nipple, then licked her lips in invitation.

He had no idea what spell she had on him. Shocked, intrigued, he heard himself breathe, "Do it again." She took her time licking her breast and areola. He couldn't imagine what it felt like.

"Watch." She winked, then took her entire nipple in her mouth and sucked herself with gusto.

"Oh fuck, Charly." Grabbing her hips, he steadied her and slammed into her even harder.

Sure, he'd had his randy days in the past. Those few years the two of them were in-between a relationship with one another, he'd played the field. But at no time in those wild, devil-may-care days filled with baseball and sex, had he been as turned on as right now, with the woman he loved.

The two of them had definitely *fucked* in the past, but this moment was well beyond that—more than illicit, this coupling would make even the most prolific of porn connoisseurs blush.

She let her breast to drop from her mouth then reached out to grasp his arms to steady herself slightly. Andy held her tighter, the flesh beneath his fingers growing white with the fierceness of his grip.

The only sound besides their moans and near screams was the loud slap of flesh on flesh. *Hard.*

"Dear God, Andy!"

Terrified of the physical response running roughshod through her system, she held on the best she could. Her mind spun, dizzy, pinpoints of light flashed in front of her eyes. Rigid with spasms, she was ready to pass out. Never before had an orgasm of such magnitude overtaken her.

And it wouldn't fucking stop!

"Help me," she thought she heard herself say. Paralyzed, she rode him and the waves of erotic elation, until she could no more, collapsing on him, internally still vibrating like a giant tuning fork had been whacked against a rock and slammed far up into her pussy, reverberating through her entire being.

Out of control, she was suddenly on her back. He collected her, steadying her, yet still pistoning severely in and out of her. As her body continued to convulse, tears covered her face.

As he continued to move, lips caressed her cheeks, clearing her tears. "Hold tight, baby, hold on tight." He brought her even closer in his hold, corralling a knee in the crook of his elbow.

His growls of near orgasm sounded animalistic. She squealed in re-arousal and near fear as he continued pounding into her. Her name roaring through the opulent hotel room, her husband came in a way she'd never experienced before. He swore, ground himself into her even deeper, shivered, arched back, then went totally silent and immensely still. Until his numbing cinch of her body relaxed and he fell on to his back and out of her.

An exceptional specimen of a human being, in better physical shape than most men his age, still he panted like an octogenarian running a marathon. Out of breath and out of energy, he sighed, "What the fuck was that, Charly?"

Cuddling him, feeling his heavy breath rise and fall against her bare skin, she licked his ear. "I don't know, but whenever you're ready, we can do it again!"

***

She left him alone in the shower, as much as they both wanted to continue this evening of more sex than they'd ever had together, after so many orgasms and physical play, any semblance of energy had been drained from them both. They'd contemplated staying the night, but they both wanted to be home with their girls, for so many reasons—the most important one, as much as they were in love with one another, they were equally as smitten with their two children.

She smiled, content. It seemed they were back on track, on the same page, in the same book. Sitting on the edge of the bed, she felt a reconnection to the man she loved and recovery from the past eight, lousy months. She prayed their love was beginning anew.

Toweling her hair, wandering the suite, she waited for Andy to finish cleaning up. She thought about the recent events of this evening—his lingering touches, his compliments, his surprise gifts. And, if they'd been caught by law enforcement in the elevator up to this suite, they'd have been charged with public indecency and lewd and lascivious conduct violations. She giggled to herself, entertaining thoughts of a bizarre Sentinel newspaper headline and a smirking Milwaukee County lockup mug shot.

She collected her clothing, folding what wouldn't be worn, tucking it away in a travel bag that *just happened* to be in the room. *Lately, you think of everything, honey!* Sitting on the bed, she began to dress, her attire much less formal than that in which she arrived. *It's going to look very odd leaving this fancy place in sweat pants.* She did the same with his clothes, when something caught her eye, a heavy linen, cream-colored envelope peeking slightly from her husband's tux jacket.

Did it pertain to this evening? Was it the leftover invitation and seating marker from their table? Why he loved to collect these little mementos from these upscale to-dos, she didn't know, but it was so inherently *him*.

Was it about *this* "date," or perhaps *another* Andy had taken? Her mind raced back to a terribly strange conversation with her friend and employer. *Paul had a nearly identical envelope. It was so odd, that's why I remember it. Some hook up service. Why would he be looking for a hook up? I might be all wrong about being back on the same page, maybe this whole evening is some giant kiss off, one last good fuck for the road, maybe this is over.*

She did her best forcing away the notion of it being anything but innocent correspondence. This evening of long, wanting looks, inconspicuous public touches, and inferred whispers had eventually brought them to this place and a night of erotic passion neither of them had experienced before. *He loves me. I know that...well, I think I do.*

Then the one irritating, irrational thought, the pissed-off concern she'd been bothered by most of the year poked her right between the eyes. Add in the cream parchment against tucked in his dark gray coat, and the worst case scenario popped out from behind every rational thought.

Shaking her head, she did the best to shake off the speculation. *He's not a cheater in any way...not at all. He loves me and the girls. He wants to be back in Milwaukee, I just need to bide my time and wait till more trade talk surfaces. He can write his own ticket anywhere at this point.*

"Babe?" A towel snugly tucked in about his waist, he sat beside his wife.

Fuck me. How can I be concerned with shit that doesn't exist when that fucking sexy, well-cut line of his hip is pointing toward his incredible cock?

"What is it, honey?"

He brushed her cheek—a warm, strong, caring touch—just like everything he had been the entire evening. That tiny gesture flung her in to a fit of insensible sobs.

"Baby."

She only cried harder when he wrapped her up in his arms.

"What is it?"

Pointing a chair, where his jacket relaxed as if nothing was amiss, she hiccuped. "That envelope. Where did you get it?"

Time to come clean, Knox!

Andy shook his head, amused as well as concerned. "Baby," he chuckled," you gotta relax." Kissing the top of her head, he left her only for a moment to retrieve the stationary from his coat. "C'mere." Encouraging her farther up on the bed, they sat cross-legged, face to face, among the rumpled linens. He handed her a tissue from a nearby box. He hadn't seen her cry with such sadness since that moment in New York, before they were married, the time he'd nearly fucked things up for good. He understood why Titan pinstripes frightened her so; she was afraid she would lose him to the wilds and seduction of the Big Apple.

Settling next to her, he dropped his head, embarrassed, afraid to look her in the eye during this confession. "I didn't know how to make sure you knew just how much I love you, how much I'm *in love* with you. We seemed so far apart this year, and I understand some of the reasons why—your trepidation and concern about New York. And I know I had to do something, *anything* to fix this." A tear slid down his cheek, he lifted his face to look in her eyes. "I hired a *professional*, I guess you could call it. Someone who could look at our situation from the outside in and give me some ideas about how to reconnect, get back on the same page with you. Because I was afraid I was losing *you.*"

He placed the parchment envelope in her hands.

Slowly, she unfolded the envelope that had tossed her into an emotional tizzy. The stationery bore a telling heading: Madame Eve, 1Night Stand. *It is—it's the same place Paul called!* Extracting the paperwork, leafing through the pages, more and more confusion darted through her mind. "Andy, this is for people who want sex—a one-night stand."

He nodded agreeing, "You're right, but sometimes a one-night stand can turn into a lifesaver. I couldn't do this on my own, Charly. I couldn't realize what I had 'let go' in our relationship, being doting, and complimentary, and like I said, sharing my fears with you." He put his forehead to hers. "You know this is how Rupp and his fiancée met. So, the next time we see him, we need to say thank you, big time! He pushed me in this direction." He kissed her gently. "You can read all that later, if you want, but I messed up big time this year and had no idea, I mean *no idea,* of how to fix it. You're so much more than I am, so out of my league, I still don't know why you said yes to marrying me."

"Because I'm in love with you."

"Do you have any idea what a *catch* you are? I know it's your job, but in the back of my mind, especially since I was gone most of the summer, I was waiting for some quadrillionaire art collector who speaks Spanish, French, and Italian, just like you do, to snatch you up and fly you to Florence or wherever on his private jet. I'm just a farm kid from Wisconsin who plays baseball and guitar."

He closed his eyes, kissing her palm as her fine hand stroked his face. "We got so many things *right* in our relationship, especially those two little beautiful monsters at home, but there were things I let fall by the wayside, like supporting you, being *your* fan as much as you are mine. Complimenting you on everything you do, especially how you pick up the slack when I'm away and even more so this season. Sometimes I didn't make you a priority, hon, and just take you out to show you off—trust me, that *will* change." He winked. "You're my best friend and I didn't share everything I should have. Did you have any idea how terrified I was of falling on my face in New York? I was so concerned about you being alone, and I missed you and the girls terribly. I didn't make that clear, and for that, and so much more this year, I am so sorry."

She collected him into her embrace, comforting him like she always had and would.

"Look at me, a big, strong, ball-busting jock crying like a baby, because I can't even scratch the surface when it comes to telling you how much I care about you and love you, Charly. You're everything to me."

"Oh, Andy."

She kissed him gently on the mouth, resting her forehead against his.

"I have to ask, baby. Where did you get that, um, *thing* you did with your breast?"

"That would be none of your business," she teased.

Rolling her in the sheets, he smothered her with kisses. "*Please* tell me you'll do it again sometime."

"Oh, you're gonna have to beg for it now…I'm going to make you wait until you're no longer wearing those ugly Titan pinstripes."

Leaning over, he dug in the bedside table drawer. Again, sitting next to her he placed a white shirt box in her hands. It was secured with a dark blue ribbon, decorated with waves and capital Ms, the color and logo of their beloved Milwaukee Breakers. "You're going to have to pay up sooner than you think."

She looked at him, unsure. After all the love-making, tears, honest discussion, and secure reconnecting, what more could there be? "What is it?"

"Not only Madame Eve tops in relationship fixing and marriage enhancing, but she has some sort of pull with Major League Baseball. Consider it an early Christmas present."

Tugging on the ribbons, opening the box, she moved tissue paper aside. The back of a white baseball jersey greeted her, KNOX in dark blue trimmed in tan stared up at her, the familiar number 27 below in matching font and hue. She shrugged, confused.

He touched her chin, needing her undivided attention. "I'm home, darlin'. Traded back. At least a five year deal. *This* whole year some sort of grand, not-so-successful experiment. You *know* the flak management took over the lousy swap with New York."

Happy tears flowed as she tossed her arms around him. "Really, you're a Breaker again?"

Taking her face in his hands, kissing her lovingly on the mouth, he smiled, content, ready for their life to be happy and complete again, here at home in Wisconsin. "It's all done but the paperwork. I'm home, honey, safe at home."

About the Author

Wendy is a born and bred Cheesehead, currently displaced for the past thirty years from her home state of Wisconsin. She works the Badger State into her stories wherever it seems to fit. During the day, she taps away at a computer in a television newsroom as a show producer, after which she does a few hours of radio. Sometimes the vocations of television, radio and romance writing cross - whoops! When not writing, you can find her lurking on Facebook, Twitter and other parts of the internet. Send her a nasty email if you like - wendyburke1994@bex.net. When not playing with the people in her head, she has silly life with her way-too-cute chef husband and three furry feline kids in the Great Lakes area of the Midwest.

Book List

For Me

Haste Ye Back

Respite

The One He Chose

Wise Men Say

19817846R00053

Printed in Great Britain
by Amazon